RAPIER WIT

By

Jennifer Oakley Denslow

Copyright 2021 by Jennifer Oakley Denslow

ISBN 979-8663012669

ALL RIGHTS RESERVED

No part of this book may be reproduced by any means, graphic, electronic, or mechanical, including photocopying, recording, taping, or by any information retrieval system without written permission from the author except in brief quotations embedded in reviews.

This is a work of fiction. The names, characters, and incidents are products of the writer's imagination. Any resemblance to persons living or dead is coincidental.

Cover illustration by L1graphics

For Keith, who keeps feeding me ideas

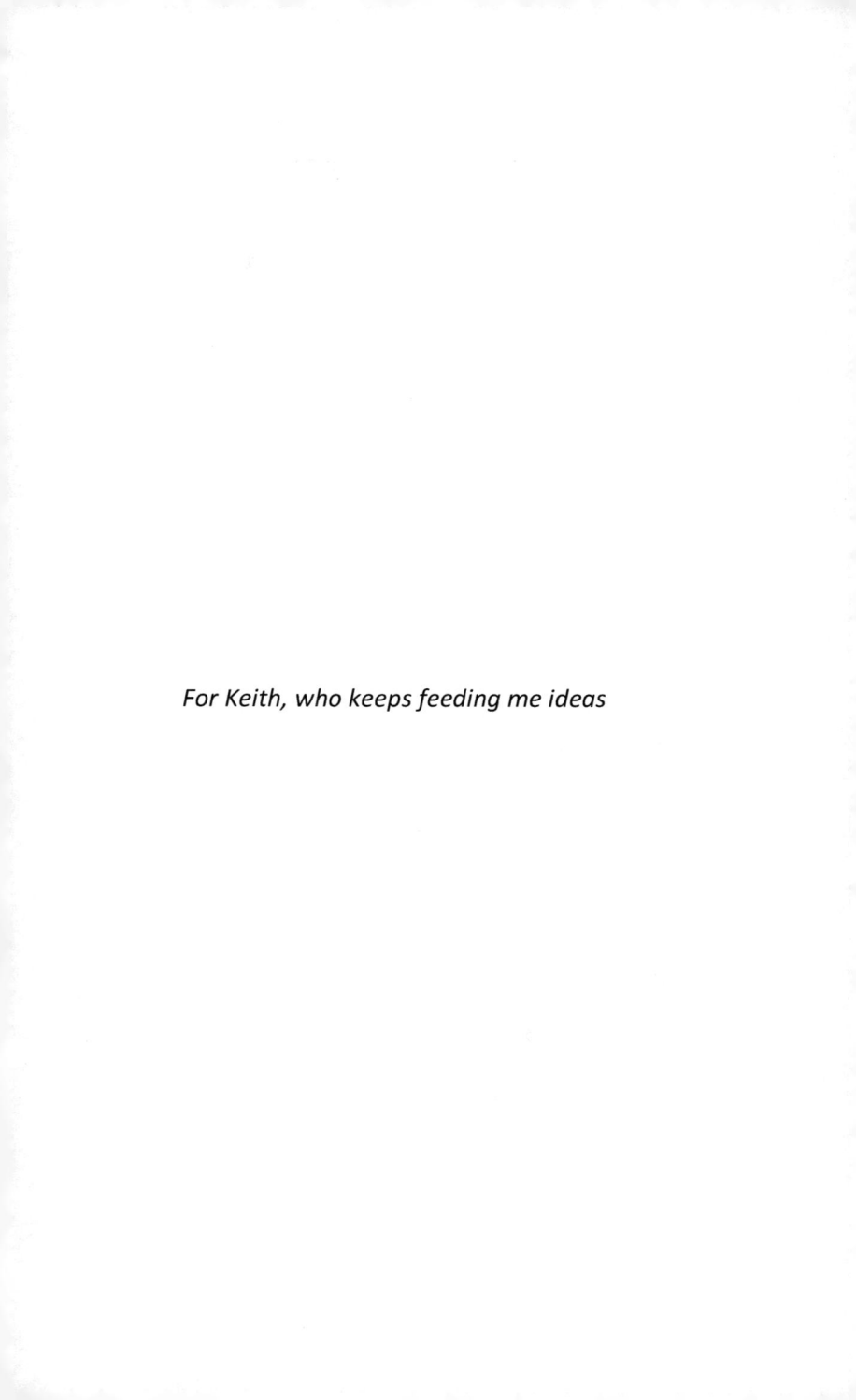

CHAPTER ONE

"Places! You know where we left off!"

Romeo and Benvolio crossed to their spots, and the others scattered to get ready for entrances or study lines. My lead actor stood with his arms thrust out as if he were putting on a straitjacket. I'd cast a young blond version of Keanu Reeves as Romeo. He flipped his hair out of his eyes with a practiced twitch and began to speak, but I interrupted him.

"I thought we agreed, Chris, you'd deliver that line as you walked across the stage."

Romeo might swagger, but I didn't think he would affect the California amble Chris used. His move from San Diego to our little town just outside Tulsa, Oklahoma, transplanted him, but it had not turned him into a cowboy. He moved like a surfer just out of the water; the boys born and raised in Quanah walked as if they'd abandoned their horses minutes before entering the auditorium.

"But Ms. M, I have a hard time doing that without tripping. Don't you think I should pace first, like he's thinking or something?" Again, he flipped his sandy hair out of his eyes, but it fell back. Arms akimbo, he added, "He's really hung up on that Rosaline chick."

"'Chick'? Isn't any of this timeless language rubbing off on you? No pacing; this play is not a tennis match. Try again. Cross back upstage and start with Romeo's speech."

He picked up the line, and I encouraged him.

"That's right. Read with the punctuation. Don't get trapped in a sing-song rhythm."

We ran through the scene in the garden, and then I focused on the scene at Capulet's house. Before long, we added Mercutio and Romeo's other buddies. In the auditorium, time seemed irrelevant, suspending us in dim amber. A good two hours later a small voice startled me out of Verona and back into the real world.

"Ms. Murphy, do you have a moment?"

I turned to find Libby Hoffman at my elbow. If it had just been us, Libby would have called me "Reg" like all the other teachers did, but in front of students she was keeping our interaction formal. Chris still paced around the stage, referring to the paperback copy of the play we were using for our production.

"Sorry to interrupt you. I found a book with gorgeous illustrations for you for costume reference." Quanah High's history teacher shoved a huge, dusty volume at me. The pale band holding her hair back in a hasty ponytail almost disappeared in the graying blonde curls. "I don't know how you can teach six classes a day and then spend three or four more hours with another group."

"Rehearsal is the best part of my day. I enjoy this." Few of my friends understood why, but Libby was an educator, so she might. I once heard a workshop presenter say elementary teachers taught because they loved kids and high school teachers because they loved their subject. I remembered her words because I believed them.

"Yes, I suppose you do." Libby looked at me as if I needed careful supervision. "I dabbled a little in theater in high school." She dipped her head and inspected her short unpolished nails.

Since she rarely shared anything about her past, her revelation surprised me. Libby seemed too shy for the stage. A role behind the scenes might fit her retiring personality. But even if she had worked backstage, costuming would not have been her strength. I always worried that the kids would volunteer her for some make-your-teacher-over show. She wore an assortment of neutral earth-tone outfits made of fibers that could be tossed into a salad as easily as woven into clothing.

I was no "after" picture myself. The most flamboyant thing about me was the red hair I frequently wrestled into submission. Other than that, I tended to pick conservative pantsuits in grays or subdued blues. With my five-feet-eleven height, I eschewed heels yet could still project authority, so I usually wore loafers.

"You might be able to use this too." Libby dug into the cavernous canvas bag she carried over her shoulder and produced a short-hilted dagger in a jeweled sheath. "A friend of mine got it for me in Venice on one of his trips. Don't you think it might work for Juliet's scene in the tomb?"

I hesitated. I remembered a high school production of Dracula that went wrong when the stake meant to do in the Count injured one of the actors. I always tried to be cautious without sacrificing the illusions I wanted to create on stage, or any students. We'd never drawn blood, and I didn't want to start with this production.

"Oh, it's not real; it's as dull as a butter knife." Libby unsheathed the souvenir and drew it across her palm, affirming its safety. "It's a letter opener, I suppose, but the jewels give it a rich look I thought might be appropriate. Lock it up if you're worried about it, and just let her flash it around for that 'O happy dagger!' bit."

"Well, yes, it does look the part." I accepted the piece. Rick would lock it in the paint cabinet backstage right. He'd make sure no one handled it until Nicole needed it for her scene.

"If there's anything else you need, let me know," Libby said. "Have the girls all reconciled themselves to their roles?"

"Not quite. Nicole doesn't have the experience, but she was luminous when she read the sides at auditions. I couldn't give it to anybody else in good conscience." I had learned that if I didn't trust my instincts when I cast a play, the whole production could go sour. "I went through the same thing when we did *Our Town* two years ago. Every girl wanted to be Emily.

And, of course, no one believes the nurse is the better part in this play. I can't stand Juliet myself. She's the perfect tragic twit."

Libby and I turned our attention to Nicole, our Juliet, perched on the edge of the stage. Her platinum blonde hair was pulled up in a studiedly casual ponytail. She was in costume. For rehearsal. Pressed cast shirt from last year's spring play. Blue jean shorts of a modest length with a neat cuff. Flip-flops of the exact shade of purple as the shirt. Nonprescription glasses broadcasting "serious thespian," although if anyone said it, Nicole would wrinkle her nose in distaste and vehemently deny any such accusation as "nasty".

"Most of them haven't known real tragedy yet. Let's hope it takes them a while to discover what that means," Libby said.

"I guess I sound impatient with them."

"No more than any of us who make a career out of watching potential go down the drain."

"Your cynicism shocks me," I said.

I thought of Libby as an idealist. For one thing, she intended to save the planet one piece of paper at a time. Libby helped a group of students distribute bins to all the high school classrooms, and every Monday her fourth hour collected the paper to take it to the recycling center one town over. In a state dependent on fossil fuels to fund the schools we taught in, Libby drove a hybrid that sat in her driveway most days while she rode a bicycle to school. The myriad small things I saw her do in a town whose reactionary attitude about environmental threats made Libby look a bit naive.

"I'm not a habitual cynic. I still believe in them. They just haven't learned where to focus themselves, at times. Like Chris, up there," she nodded toward the actor, now absorbed in the playbook. "He should be taking the AP history exam, but is he?"

"He seems to be one who'd do well on the test. If he scored high enough, it could save him some college hours next year."

"Well, he says he's not going to school. Not yet. He's got some idea about heading to the Far East and bumming around before he submits to a classroom again."

I made a low whistle. "And how does his father feel?"

While Chris, the definition of free spirit, was an open, friendly, and intelligent boy, his father looked like the headmaster of a military academy. Robert Slayton instituted a regimented approach in his math classroom. He kept students glued to their seats working problems while he patrolled the perimeter, barking at them to keep at it.

"Well, Slayton and I aren't on the same wavelength, but I can just imagine." Libby clamped her lips together, but she couldn't contain herself and burst forth with, "the last time he thought my class was disturbing him too much, he knocked on my door to inform me it was people like me who ruined the country in the 1960s and he intended to take America back, starting with my room."

Libby was far more confident in front of her classes than she was in any social situation, and her teaching was marked by exuberant student participation. Once she greeted them at the door by saying, "This index card I'm handing you determines your caste during class today. You may not speak first to someone of a higher caste and you likely won't want to speak to anyone of a lower caste unless you give them an order."

The role-playing in Libby's class could bring world history alive for students. It could also bring parents to the school. The exercise in social order prompted a confused student to report at home that Ms. Hoffman had said she was low class and her parents were too. Who could guess what might have been going on in Libby's classroom the day Slayton tapped on her door?

"I took a year after college to work in New York," I said. "I learned a lot there, but I got a degree before I went to the city."

"A person can get themselves involved in some unimaginable stuff halfway around the world."

"Or in his own backyard."

"Yes, in his own backyard."

Libby left the auditorium, bag slung over her shoulder, as I turned back to catch up with the action onstage.

There was no action onstage.

While I was distracted, the actors had morphed from the upper crust of Verona into regular high school students. Random hammering and a few expletives from backstage signaled at least the set crew was working. I grabbed a black stretchy headband out of my bag and started twisting my hair back. The curls gave a good fight, but I finally tamed the red mass and was ready to get rehearsal back on track.

"Isn't Tybalt supposed to be here? In fact, isn't he supposed to be onstage right now?" I tried to sound calm, but missing actors complicated the process.

"Sonic called him in for a shift," one of the extras said. "I could fill in if you want me to."

I turned my head to ignore the hopeful expression of a novice who felt he'd been miscast. "I've told you to let me know about conflicts before they happen."

"Ms. Murphy," Chris said, "we're here. And we've worked hard today. I didn't even trip the last time I crossed."

"Point taken." A deep breath cleared my head and calmed me down. I inventoried what we'd accomplished. "Let's pack it in for the day. We only have about five minutes left anyway."

As I tried to stuff a day's worth of detritus into my canvas bag, Colonel Slayton's voice emanated from the rear of the auditorium.

"Am I to assume your rehearsal is over for the day?" He braced at the top of the aisle. His navy slacks held stiff, precise creases. At the end of a long day in the classroom, his white dress shirt was free of wrinkles except where his elbows bent so he could clasp his hands behind his back. The blue and white regimental stripe tie he wore hung perfectly straight from the knot cinched close to his Adam's apple.

"Yes, Colonel, it is."

"Then may I steal my son away from these pantywaist pastimes so he may join me and his mother for our evening meal?"

"Yes, that would be fine ..." I struggled, but the tenor of his voice and my mother's efforts to raise me to be a lady forced me to add a single syllable to the sentence. "Sir."

The colonel turned on his heel and left the auditorium. Chris slouched his way up the aisle after him.

"Rick, will you lock this dagger ... uhm, prop ... up before we leave? We'll use it for Juliet's scene in the tomb." As my cast scattered, I called out, "Tomorrow, we're working on the brawl in the city square."

"Won't be nothin' like the brawl at Chris's house tonight," Lab Whitney said. He joined me on the walk up the aisle.

"What do you mean?"

"Romeo might not be Romeo for too much longer. Chris said his dad is pressuring him to drop the play."

"Well, I haven't heard anything about it."

"The colonel's specialty is sneak attacks." With that enigmatic statement, Lab let loose a simulated round of machine-gun fire and picked up speed so he burst through the door like an infantryman going over a hill. I didn't stop, although the thought of losing Chris was like hitting a brick wall with my head. No one in auditions showed Chris's talent or presence. I couldn't replace him. Our football coach's description of his frustration with his varsity team fit my situation: I had no depth. If Chris hadn't transferred in, I wouldn't have decided to do *Romeo and Juliet.*

I'd deal with the problem of Chris quitting the show if it presented itself. All I'd heard was Lab's comment. I didn't doubt the colonel wanted his son to quit the play, but until Chris came to me himself, there was nothing I could do. Except grade the papers in my bag.

CHAPTER TWO

The next day, Chris's father followed him into the auditorium for rehearsal.

"My dad's staying until we finish today." Chris shrugged his shoulder toward his father, who sat in one of the seats in the back row. "He said he'll wait for me and then I won't be back in here again."

"You made a commitment to this play!"

"He wants me to quit now." Chris hunched his shoulders and looked away from me.

I shouldn't have been so quick to speak. Chris's nonverbal language telegraphed his disagreement with his dad's decision. His father had decided for him. "I'll need some time to replace you. Can you come for a few days more?"

"No." He glanced over his shoulder to his father, who had unpacked his briefcase and clicked a ballpoint pen into action. "Today has to be the last day. I can't talk to him about it anymore."

"We'll be starting right away," I called to Chris's father. He was already generously deploying red ink on the stack of papers he'd taken out to grade. He focused on the papers, completely ignoring the students gathering for rehearsal. His lack of interest in students puzzled me, but I was, like most theater teachers, invested in my students' emotional and mental health in a way many math teachers might not be.

Other teachers had conflicts with the colonel as well. A few days ago Lenore Roland, an English teacher at Quanah who was both my mentor and friend, had told me about a showdown on Hallway B, where both math and social studies classes met.

"If Libby and the colonel lived next door to each other," she'd said, "they'd always be running to court over an overhanging limb or garbage cans left out too long."

"Was she frightened?" I asked.

"When I talked to her, she was trembling, but I don't believe she was scared. Libby may seem to be a reed, but she's an iron post. Her class had been a little loud and the colonel spoke to her about the noise. End of story."

Knowing the colonel, his bark was about the same as a bite. Libby may have been intimidated by his approach.

She had come in earlier as the kids gathered for our rehearsal. I had seen her head backstage left, toward the dressing rooms, waving a bundle of material at me. The theater bug had bitten, and she was going to work on costumes. With Libby backstage and the colonel at the back of the auditorium, the neutral field between them should have been large enough for me to work on the play without distractions. Normally, I ran closed rehearsals. Unlike our basketball coaches, who always had gung ho parents in the bleachers during workouts, I wasn't used to doing my job while parents observed. I was beginning rehearsal with a knot of tension in my neck.

Chris's voice brought me back to the present.

"I tried to tell him you didn't like parents hanging out when we worked. He just laughed. I can't picture him letting Abby's folks sit in on one of his classes." Chris's hands curled into fists. "He said that's different, that math is real work and this is play."

"Well, it is," I told Chris. "The best kind of play. Everything will be okay. Your dad will get some work done while he waits. I'll try not to keep you long. I don't want to make this hard on you. Help me break in our new Romeo."

I couldn't imagine what he was feeling. His father had demanded he quit the play when he not only had the talent to excel but had committed to be a part of it as well. Chris regretted breaking his word about doing the play. But I also knew he wanted to please his father.

"My dad loves me, Ms. Murphy. He just doesn't understand me." No matter how unoriginal it sounded, Chris's plaint was real.

"I think a lot of people have felt the same way." I had nothing more comforting to offer, so I turned to the group. "Let's get started! Lab can lead warm-ups. Rick, take roll, please."

Rick opened his bulging notebook to the day's call sheet, checking off actors. The cast spread out across the stage. Lab led them through the warm-up routine. Chris participated for the last time. The colonel looked up from his grading and snorted when the group started doing Rockette-style kicks. Lab had an original approach to preparing for rehearsal.

Warm-ups completed, Lab and Chris joined a couple of other actors drifting toward center stage. I directed them back to an early scene in the play, where Romeo's friends would find him wandering in a garden. Actors scattered around the auditorium to work on lines until I needed them onstage.

"Ms. M, I don't understand why we're doing the scene in front of the curtain. Are we too cheap to build another set?" Chris paused down center to ask.

"In a word, yes. Suspend your disbelief! That blue curtain behind you is a garden, ripe with heavy flowers and lush vines." I used my hands to shape the vegetation as I described it, and several of the boys who saw what I was doing with my hands snickered. I lowered my hands quickly. "Imagine a night scene in a courtyard. You're surrounded by flowers. You smell jasmine wafting through the air. The air is almost too heavy with its perfume to breathe. Work with it."

I tried to eye the other actors as if I'd never seen them before, assessing whether any of them might step into Romeo's tights. Lab's flamboyant gestures defined the mercurial Mercutio. I couldn't see any of the other boys playing Mercutio with such verve. Romeo, with his mooning and swooning about the stage, was far easier to replace, and for that, Adam King was my best choice. In auditions, he had overread, giving the sides a melodramatic spin I didn't want onstage opening night, but he had tried to do something other than read the lines in a shaking monotone, and I appreciated that.

Adam had the right attitude too. Even after I didn't cast him, he'd been hanging around rehearsals, trying to help out the crew. I didn't have to look whenever I heard something fall backstage. It was always Adam. Usually, it wasn't Adam falling; it was Adam making things fall. Of course, Romeo didn't have to be graceful. He's a horny teenager. When you reduce him to his essence, he's a roiling container of hormones. Chris's Romeo could move across the stage without revealing all that turbulence. Adam's performance would be a contrast to Chris's. Adam was Stanley from *A Streetcar Named Desire*, and Chris was Tom from *The Glass Menagerie*.

A disturbance at the back of the auditorium distracted me, and I turned around. Forgetting it was the colonel who had camped out to grade in the seats just below the lighting booth, I yelled, "Hey, we're working down here, and I can't focus if you don't knock it off!"

Both figures froze. The colonel was standing up, and although the dim light in the rear of the auditorium hid most details, standing beside him was our high school wrestling coach, Stephen Keener. Outside the auditorium, the coach was half a foot shorter than Slayton, but here he stood at the foot of the seats and had lost another few inches in comparative stature. Keener was bulkier than Slayton. I could see his shoulders hunched and his arms held stiffly out from his body.

"Sorry about that, Reg." Stephen was the first to speak.

"I apologize, Ms. Murphy. We didn't mean to distract you or the students. Coach Keener was just leaving."

Keener stood looking up at Slayton who returned the stare until Keener shrugged, shook a finger at him, and left.

"You won't be hearing anything from me again," the colonel said, sitting back down with his pile of papers.

The doors to the auditorium closed slowly after Keener because of their pneumatic hinges, so even if he had wanted to slam them, he couldn't. His exit was unremarkable.

Turning back to the play, I called out Adam's name, and he appeared in his paint-spattered overalls and ragged T-shirt. I hoped there was more paint on the flats than there was on him.

"I need you to read for me. I may have to recast a part and I want to see how you handle being onstage." Adam nodded and took a copy of the play from Chris. I had our Benvolio, Jim, read the scene with Adam as Chris shadowed him, offering blocking advice.

A crash backstage startled me even more than usual because Adam was onstage and couldn't have been responsible for it.

"Quiet them down, Rick," I told the stage manager. He disappeared behind the stage-left curtains. I hadn't known that anyone else was left backstage working on set since Adam had stepped out under the lights.

The boys onstage were still working through the scene, and I needed to watch Adam. Was he the right choice to replace Chris?

"Dude, you've gotta get those hands up there! Anything below the waist is like chicken wings. Flapping around won't take you anywhere." Chris's instructions left me bemused. He repeated almost verbatim what he'd heard from me since the beginning of rehearsals. "And don't stomp. Stride!"

Adam proved as graceless onstage as he was as a stagehand, but his voice resonated enough to reach the back seats of the theater. Adam's awkwardness was just a different version of Chris's, and with the original actor at his shoulder, he seemed to be comfortable with the whole process.

Rick slipped into the seat beside me. "I can't find anything. The girls are sewing with Ms. Hoffman in the costume room. The set stuff is still standing backstage left. No one's there."

"Who was Adam working with?"

Rick shrugged. "They cleaned up, I guess. No one's left."

"So much for our noise problem. Something succumbed to gravity and fell. Make sure the overhead door is closed before we leave." I waved Rick away. He went to pick up his prompt book. I walked up and leaned on the lip of the stage. "Adam, you're doing a nice job. How do you feel on stage?"

"Okay, I guess. I'm used to being back there." Adam jerked a thumb toward the wings.

Chris jumped offstage and flopped into a seat in the first row, listening to my exchange with his replacement.

Nicole and Abby were making their way stage right for an upcoming balcony scene. I'd held them in reserve until I could see how Adam handled sharing the stage with Nicole. Most teenage boys are the equivalent of hormonal dynamite. A few minutes on stage with Nicole's cotton-candy blonde hair and pristine complexion might make him overheat. I could deal with problems, but I needed to know about them before we were well into rehearsal with a new Romeo.

"I need a favor. We need you in the play. Chris can't continue, and I thought you would be a good replacement."

"Will Nicole still be Juliet?" Adam blushed deep crimson at the thought.

"Yes. In fact, I want the two of you to read through the balcony scene. I need to know how you'll work together. You read the play last year in freshman English, right?"

"Yes, ma'am."

"So you know how Romeo eavesdrops on Juliet as she comes out on the balcony? You need to lurk at the base of our tower. Listen to Juliet and her nurse."

Rick interrupted, taking a seat down front by Chris. "Overhead door's closed, Murph. Lights out backstage. Someone's still in the girl's dressing room, but I didn't peek."

Adam headed for his place on stage, but instead of a conversation between the nurse and her charge, a sharp shriek and a fusillade of voices came from backstage left.

"Oh, Ms. Murphy! Somebody's back here! I don't know who it is and I think he's dead!" Abby Beamer rushed onto the stage in odd bits and pieces of her costume over her normal teen habit. She should have been comic in her wimple and blue jeans, but her face had that taut, shiny look of the terrified.

Close on her heels, our Juliet appeared, almost crashing into her.

"I'm not going back there. I think I saw blood." Nicole fluttered and stamped in excitement. "He wasn't moving."

"Go out in the house, girls. I'll take a look." Expecting to find one of the mannequins from the costume room set up to freak someone out, I ran up the steps shoved against the edge of the stage and charged backstage, flipping on the work lights as I went. Rick had been back here a few minutes ago and hadn't seen anything.

It was dim under the work lights, but I could make out the shape on the floor, half-hidden behind a stack of platforms.

The man's head flopped to one side, his arms flung out in an extravagant gesture as if he were surrendering to the inevitable. Stepping closer, I took in gray buzz-cut hair and staring eyes. A dark, shiny pool of liquid pooled underneath his head. This was no mannequin.

The lights dimmed and then flashed bright again. My head buzzed. I spread my arms out for support, but found nothing to grab. I sat down on the floor, hard, and recognized the colonel.

The man sprawled on the concrete was the colonel.

The body count for *Romeo and Juliet* wasn't as high as some of Shakespeare's plays. Hamlet, for instance, had dead bodies all over the stage by the time the curtain closed. But in theater, the dead weren't truly dead. The corpses weren't supposed to be real.

The metallic fragrance from the blood beneath the colonel's head was sharper than the sweet aroma of the corn syrup in the fake blood we used in plays. I gagged a little. I reached out a hand for support, leaned on the concrete floor, and closed my eyes against the jittering room.

My senses returned to normal; the world steadied. My stomach still felt queasy. I forced myself to inch toward the body and reach out to feel for a pulse. I had to shuffle closer on my knees before I could touch his wrist.

Nothing.

Under stress, I tended to slow down so I could think rationally, but I didn't have time to think everything out and then act when students might still be at risk. If someone had attacked the colonel, then the same person might be lurking here in the auditorium. I had to lead the kids somewhere safe. I pushed off the floor and stepped out from the curtains toward the students milling around on stage with Nicole and Abby.

"Rick, call 911," I said, pointing to my stage manager. He could take care of that while I tried to sort out what to do with the kids. Rick pulled out his cell phone and began dialing, sprinting out of the auditorium to find better reception. Without thinking, I herded the students down the steps in front of the stage, making sure Chris was among them.

The colonel was beyond help, and it looked like it had been more than an accident. Nothing backstage looked out of place.

Other than the body.

I pushed away the image of the colonel, prone on the concrete floor with a pool of red blood under his head, and tried not to hypothesize further. The women in the murder mysteries I read might find that their minds immediately begin to churn with possibilities, but I was here, in real life, with a dead body and a group of teenagers to protect. I wanted to make them join hands like a chain of preschoolers because I couldn't hold their hands individually.

"Circle up!" I said, drawing them into the shape we always stood in for warm-ups before a show. "Someone has had an accident backstage. We need to move out to the lobby. Leave your things."

Most of the students had cell phones in their hands, but everyone left backpacks and the outerwear they'd thrown across seats when they'd arrived. Every one of us held what was once a computer that would have taken up an entire room at one time, but we were traveling light. Funny what random ideas occurred to me.

Maybe I was in shock.

Maybe I needed medical attention.

I steered my thoughts back to the students and ushered them up the aisle, out the door, across the carpeted auditorium lobby, and into the tiled foyer.

"Murphy, what's going on?" Lab asked me.

"I don't think I can answer that question," I said. I decided it would be wise to keep quiet about details so I wouldn't compromise law enforcement's work. "Let's hang out until we know what we need to do."

"I'm going to need my backpack," Nicole said. She'd stopped right beside me outside the auditorium doors. "I've got to read another chapter of *The Great Gatsby* for AP tonight."

"You'll get your backpack before you leave, I'm sure." Nicole's nonchalance shocked me; she had seen the body backstage. I wanted to ask her if she understood we were in the middle of a crime scene but stayed quiet.

"Well, none of us had anything to do with whatever happened backstage. We'd probably be better off leaving. That hobo or whoever it was might come after us next." Several of her friends nodded in agreement with Nicole's analysis. Abby didn't join in but stood with her head down, breathing heavily.

"We'll be fine. We have to wait for the sheriff to show up and let us know if we can go. We're in a well-lit place with windows and glass doors people can see through. No one is going to harm us here in broad daylight." I sounded so convincing I even calmed myself.

"I have to go back there. I've had CPR training. I can help." Chris tried to push past me, back into the auditorium.

"Sit with the others while we sort everything out." I steered him toward the rest of the cast and crew, who all sat on the tile floor of the foyer, leaning against walls or each other. "The best thing is to wait out here with everybody else."

"Where's my dad? He was here when rehearsal started. You talked to him," Chris said. He sat down by Lab. "I don't see him anywhere now. He's disappeared."

I weighed the consequences of telling Chris his dad had been the victim, and decided he needed to know. Better to hear it from me than to overhear it if one of the other kids figured it out or the sheriff announced it once he arrived.

"I think your father is backstage."

Chris relaxed. "Oh, yeah. Good. He'll know what to do."

Lab looked at me and then at Chris. "I think what she means is—"

"I think your father is who I found backstage."

"What?" Chris's face blanked and then he tried to get up, grabbing Lab's shoulder for support. "We really need to go, then. He'll need our help."

Lab grabbed the hand Chris placed on his shoulder but stayed silent, looking to me to say what had to be said.

"We can't help him, Chris. It's too late. He's gone."

Chris sagged and turned away from us, leaning his head against the wall, his shoulders shaking. My instinct was to pull him into a hug, away from the cinder block wall, until his mother arrived and gathered him to her for comfort.

"My phone didn't have a signal, so I used the office phone, but the dispatcher said someone's on the way." Rick rejoined us. The sirens nearing the school underlined the stage manager's report.

CHAPTER THREE

I mentally planted my feet and prepared myself for his questions when I saw our principal, Bart Lincoln, push his way out of the front office doors into the foyer.

"Ms. Murphy, what is going on in here? This young man came down to my office to call 911. Is someone injured?" Lincoln shouted. The idea to hold this conversation out of the students' earshot hadn't occurred to him.

"You could say that," I muttered to myself. I thought if I stayed quiet and low key, Lincoln would read the nonverbal signals and come close enough for the two of us to talk without being overheard. I started toward him, hoping to meet him halfway.

"Is it one of the students? Whose parents should I be calling?" He still didn't move.

"The victim is a parent. A teacher." Speaking under my breath, I tried to convey a sense of discretion without resorting to telling my principal to shut up before the kids freaked out. "The colonel is hurt. Rick called for help, and I've gathered all the students right here."

"Why aren't you back there with the colonel, helping him until the paramedics arrive?" Bart's question was reasonable, but his dismissal of my judgment in this crisis poked me like a stick.

"He's beyond any kind of help I could give him." I didn't want to go into detail about why I couldn't do anything. The colonel had been warm to the touch, but so still when I reached for his nonexistent pulse.

My comment stopped Lincoln for a moment.

I glanced back at the kids by the auditorium doors. Chris still rested against the wall, and Lab stood by him, patting his shoulder. Most of the girls had gathered in a tight circle, chattering and checking their phones, except Abby. She stood apart from the others, her shoulders jerking with rapid, shallow breaths. Her face was the color of cream of chicken soup straight out of the can.

"Abby, calm down. Put your head between your knees and breathe, for heaven's sake!" I called to her. I knew Lab was going to say something crude about my instructions, and I didn't want to hear it. I turned back to finish my conversation with Lincoln. Before I could speak, I heard someone rap on the glass doors. Outlined in the glow from the lights along the sidewalk was Mac Snyder, our county sheriff.

Either the sheriff really knew how to make an entrance, or I was still shocky from discovering the colonel. The figure haloed in the door seemed ten feet tall.

Bart lumbered over and opened the door.

"I understand there's been a disturbance. The ambulance is on the way." Mac squinted at me as he moved closer, but it didn't make him look menacing, just focused. "Tell me what we've got."

"Someone is dead backstage." As I said it out loud, I felt dizzy. "I brought the kids out here right away. I've accounted for them all. My stage manager called for help as soon as we discovered the colonel. I'm glad you're here."

"I'll have to go check it out myself. Stay here, and don't let anyone wander off." Mac followed the two EMTs trundling a stretcher through the glass door and into the auditorium. He left briefly and came back out where Bart and I still stood.

I glanced at the students. Most were talking on their cell phones, spreading the word about our discovery. Information, conjecture, and flat-out lies oozed through Quanah's teenage communication web, and there wasn't a dam strong enough to hold it back.

"The kids are a little shaken up," I said when Mac rejoined us.

"Of course. You can hand this crew over to me." He raised his voice to speak to the students. "I'm going to have to ask you guys a few questions. You hold still while I talk to you one at a time. I'll start with Ms. Murphy here."

"Sheriff, a basketball game is about to start, and I'm calling it," Bart said. "I'll speak to you before you leave."

When he left, Mac took me aside. Nicole interrupted us almost immediately.

"Sheriff! Sheriff! I don't think my parents would appreciate you interrogating me." Nicole sniffed. "I had absolutely nothing to do with whatever happened."

"Then there'll be very few questions. I'll get you out of here real soon. And I'm sure your daddy will understand." Mac led me toward one end of the stage. One of the EMTs stuck his head out from the auditorium. Mac looked up as the technician shook her head and then disappeared.

"Maybe we could move everybody out of the way, Sheriff," I said.

"Just call me Mac." He ignored my suggestion. "What happened here, Ms. Murphy?"

"Call me Reg. Short for Regina." I tried to stay civil while I pressed him on the issue. Even though the kids knew what was going on, they shouldn't have to see the colonel's body being trundled out by the EMTs. "I'm not sure you want them all to be here when they remove Colonel Slayton."

"Good point, Reg. Let's move up by the office."

Herding students to the opposite end of the lobby proved easier than I expected. About a dozen of them had been at rehearsal.

"We were practicing," I said. "I was talking to a couple of the actors onstage. Two of the girls ran onto the stage screaming, and when I went backstage, I found the colonel sprawled on the floor."

"Did you do anything for him?" Lincoln's questions earlier were an interrogation. Mac's questions sounded like genuine concern, for me and for the colonel.

"I felt for a pulse and didn't find one. I got the kids together and had our stage manager call 911."

"Do we have everybody here who was present at the time?" Mac pulled a cheap spiral-bound memo pad and pen out of his shirt pocket.

"Yes, I think so. Rick's our stage manager. He'll have a call list." Mac frowned at the unfamiliar term, so I added, "A list of everyone who was supposed to be here today. I'll give you a copy."

"The people on that list would be the only people who were in the auditorium during your rehearsal?"

"Yes. I don't let people just hang out at rehearsals." A good thing I didn't. Look what had happened to the colonel. I shuddered at how close we had all been to death this afternoon. I imagined a gray-robed and hooded figure tapping me on the shoulder, but Mac's next question chased the image out of my head.

"Any adults here, other than you or the colonel?" He still hadn't taken any notes, but bounced the writing end of his pen on the small spiral-topped notebook, creating a galaxy of little dots like stars on the blue-lined paper.

"No. The colonel was here to wait for Chris. Usually parents aren't around, and I'm the production team."

"You, the colonel, and what, a dozen teenagers?"

I realized someone was missing. "And Libby."

"Libby?"

"Libby Hoffman, our history teacher. I'd forgotten. She was here earlier, working on costumes. She must have slipped out while we were running scenes."

Mac made a note and meditated on it. The students were getting restless, and I glared at them to bring the noise level down. Nicole was engaged in an animated conversation on her cell phone. Abby was still pasty and sweaty. Shock? Chris sat with his head in his hands. The others were a little stunned but looked normal.

Scanning the faces of my students calmed me. Every time my mind wandered back to the colonel's body lying backstage, the blood drained from my head and pooled in my stomach. Mac's voice stilled my dizziness.

"How did she leave without you noticing?" Mac asked me.

"Easily. If we're working, my attention is on the kids. I didn't even know the colonel was backstage. I wouldn't notice if Libby slipped up one of the side aisles and out the doors back there. And she wouldn't have thought to interrupt just to say she was leaving." I usually appreciated such consideration, but now it seemed perverse that she wouldn't let me know she was going home for the day.

"Uh-huh. And is that the only way out of the auditorium?" He nodded at the door we'd all gone through to the lobby.

"Oh, no." Closing my eyes, I turned around as I spoke so I could place all the doors that led out of the huge space. "Two sets of double doors at the head of each of the two center aisles, a door out each side midway up the house. Another door out stage left by the dressing rooms, a door out stage right from the scene shop, a door at the top of the steps on both sides of the stage, and then the overhead door at the back of stage right. That was open for a while today, but Rick shut it before we found the colonel."

"So it was wide open? Would you say for most of the rehearsal?"

I nodded.

"All the other doors were locked, aside from the lobby door and the overhead door?"

"The doors lock from the outside. But sometimes the kids prop them open to make it easier to slip in and out. I don't know if the backstage exits are open or not. I haven't been back there today."

"Except when you found the colonel."

I nodded. My throat tightened and my eyes burned just thinking about how he'd looked sprawled on the floor backstage.

"So someone else may have wandered in." Mac's paper had more of his sharp printing on it now that I'd answered some of his questions. He'd even sketched a rough little map of the auditorium while I was twirling around. "I'll need to talk to Miss Libby after I finish here."

"Yes." I thought about what his question implied. Had one of us hurt the colonel? Or had someone random wandered backstage to attack? Neither possibility comforted me.

"Well, that news complicates my job. I'm going to have a heck of a time securing this place and keeping an eye on these kids without some help." He tapped his pen on the notepad again, thinking. "I need to talk to 'em and get them on out of here if they're not involved. You keep them corralled, and I'll go survey the scene back there again while I call Shrimp in."

Great. Calling in his deputy. Shrimp was the last person I wanted to see right now. His sniffing officiousness made my skin crawl, and we had recently been out on a particularly unsuccessful date.

I approached the kids when Mac entered the auditorium.

"We're all upset. The sheriff has a protocol to follow to keep us safe and find out what happened here." It was oddly easy to get the students' attention. Every pair of eyes was on me, and the majority of them had closed their phones to listen. "We're going to make sure the sheriff's job isn't made any more difficult by our behavior. I suggest you pull out something to study. Say, lines for the play, maybe? Or, for those of you who have my English class, tomorrow is vocab day. We'll just wait until Shrimp—I mean—Deputy Standfield gets here and the sheriff can finish up his questioning."

"Ms. Murphy, should I call my mom?" Chris's eyes were red-rimmed and tense.

"You must want to be with her. Let me call her," I said. Chris shouldn't have to tell his mother her husband was dead.

He nodded and reached his hand out like a toddler groping for a grown-up's hand to cross the street. I took it, and we stood there to take a deep breath before we darted out among the traffic.

31

CHAPTER FOUR

I stood with Chris until his mom arrived. I didn't know what to say. We leaned against the lobby wall opposite the front doors of the school. I could hear Chris's breath as he struggled to keep from crying.

Some adolescent code kept him from breaking down in public. Instead, he held his breath and tightened his face until the tension must have made his stomach roll. When he found himself alone, would he give in and weep? Or would the time he spent tamping down the tears compact them so much he couldn't do anything but lie in his bed and wonder why his muscles ached?

Ginny Slayton arrived a few minutes after I called her. She came through the double glass doors to the lobby and to Chris like iron filings fly at a magnet. The two of them embraced and I rubbed my hand where Chris's grip had reddened it.

"Ms. Murphy, thank you for looking out for Chris," Ginny spoke to me after they had moved apart. Their hands twined together. Her face tensed as she asked, "Should I go in to see?"

"Oh, no, they've taken him already. I don't think you need to go in there."

"I'm sorry I couldn't get here right away. Thursdays are my day to work in the yard, and I was out back when the phone rang. Who was it?" She looked at Chris.

"I called, Mom."

"Yes, it was you." Ginny balled up her fist against her thin, pale lips and shook her head, composing herself. "So silly of me to get mixed up."

"At a time like this, it's completely understandable."

"I'll take Chris home, and we'll see what needs to be done."

"Are you okay driving, Mrs. Slayton?" I asked her. She spoke coherently, but her face was pale and her eyes were wide and rabbity.

"Fine. I'm just fine. I want to get Chris home. Will you tell the sheriff we've gone?" She led Chris out the door before I could answer.

Mac returned not long after Ginny and Chris left.

"You let them leave."

I stuttered under his gaze. "They were so upset, Sheriff. I don't think I could have kept them here."

"The two people closest to the victim and they walked out the door. I'm going to have to talk to both of them." Mac shook his head. "I thought you understood ..."

"You didn't deputize me. Everyone is doing the best they can under the circumstances."

"You're right. I'm sorry about that, Ms. Murphy. I'm so used to giving orders and wrangling people to do their jobs, I forgot for a minute you weren't one of my deputies." Mac blushed as he apologized. The tension I'd felt when he chastised me subsided a bit as he continued. "I'll send someone over and take care of the crime-scene business here after I talk to the rest of the kids and get headed home." He turned his back on me and pulled out his cell phone. I couldn't overhear much, but I assumed he was sending someone over to meet the Slaytons.

Mac questioned everyone still present, releasing them as he got the answers he needed. He tracked down Mr. Lincoln to establish the principal's whereabouts during the rehearsal. Parents came in intermittently to ferry their kids home. I stayed to hold hands and help find rides home for the dwindling number of students left.

CHAPTER FIVE

At nearly midnight, I pulled into my driveway.

Walking through my door, I paused and closed my eyes to enjoy the silence for a moment. A rustle from the living room caught my attention.

Gus, my large, orange cat, refused to meet me at the door. His tail brushed against the magazines piled on the coffee table where he posed and stared. He didn't need a voice to communicate his displeasure. I'd missed filling his bowl for his second meal of the day.

The light on my answering machine was blinking. I punched the button to play back the messages and listened while I filled Gus's bowl with dry food and a dollop of canned chicken. He loved tuna, but tuna didn't love him, so, since the vet had recommended it, he got chicken instead of "chicken of the sea."

My mother had not heard the news, so her message was brief. Crews from the Tulsa television stations would be massing outside the school by the morning, and Mom would hear about it then. On one hand, if I talked to her tonight, I could forestall any frantic calls of concern. On the other hand, this late, she would be asleep. I'd wait to call her in the morning and hope that she hadn't turned on her television before I reached her.

Most of the other messages were variations of "let me know if I can help" and "hang in there, kid" from other teachers at Quanah.

Our Family and Consumer Science teacher, Helen Miller, had called. Helen's name was right above mine on the calling tree we used to contact each other in case something happened at the school. The message she left told me Bart Lincoln had scheduled a faculty meeting in the morning before class.

Lincoln had made that decision fast. I was a little amused to think of the criticism he would face. Such a decision meant he wouldn't have to negotiate the precarious line between those who would want the school closed because of Slayton's death and those who demanded the school doors stay open. Lincoln chose to keep the school open and by doing so named his enemies.

For once, I supported Lincoln's decision. We needed to be in school on Friday. The school was its own support system. The students would have their friends, and we had a crisis plan that brought counselors from our district together with clergy from the local churches to be there for the kids who needed someone to listen. Having class and trying to act normal on an extraordinary day would be difficult, but we'd be there for our students.

After the last message, I took off my jacket and headed for my bedroom at the back of the house to change into my favorite flannel pajamas. The pair I'd pulled out from the cedar chest at the foot of the bed was so old and so often washed that the two pieces felt softer than rabbit fur. Three small pearly buttons kept the fly on the gray flannel bottoms closed, and the waist had a drawstring that pulled tight enough to hold them up but not tight enough to bind. The matching top featured the same buttons down the front, a notched collar with red piping, and a print featuring fortune cookies and random Chinese characters.

In the kitchen, I filled a kettle with water and set it on the burner to boil. Satiated, Gus made up with me by curling around my ankles. I tried not to step on him as I pulled a mug and an envelope of hot chocolate mix from the cabinet. I reflected on how many times we had been working on a show and I thought, "This schedule is going to kill me."

One rehearsal had been fatal for the colonel.

I didn't want to be in the middle of a murder investigation, and I didn't want to worry that the colonel's murder was somehow connected to our play.

Or the cast and crew.

What if the person who attacked the colonel meant to go after someone in the play and only killed the colonel because he got in the way? Was it possible that one of the teenagers involved in the cast or crew was homicidal as well as hormonal? Students didn't like the colonel because of his stringent classroom rules, but disliking a teacher was a weak motive for murder. I knew, though, that what seems minor to an adult can seem immense to an adolescent. Following that logic, the colonel could have been the wrong victim and the perpetrator was after someone else for what might be an insignificant reason.

I tried to stay analytical, but the longer I thought about it, the more I kept seeing flashes of the scene backstage. The colonel's vacant, staring eyes and his hands, thrown up in what appeared to be surprise, floated in my vision alongside images of my students. We had been so close to death, and I felt sick at the thought of how badly I had failed at keeping rehearsal safe. Every student had made it home, but they had all come so close to the murder. I shook, thinking about what might have happened if one of them had encountered the murderer when he was attacking the colonel.

The kettle on my stove shrieked, startling me. The boiling water gave me a distraction; I mixed up some hot chocolate and cuddled up on the couch with an afghan, a gift from my grandmother. I intended to give my brainwaves a rest and clicked the remote to find something streaming on Netflix.

My mind kept wandering back to the afternoon in the auditorium. After the emotional upheaval of finding the colonel's body, Mac's methodical approach and quiet quest for answers had been a relief.

My eyes drooped, and the sound from the television blurred. The hot chocolate was soothing. I could feel myself relaxing as I sipped it. Then the doorbell rang. I went to the door and peeped out one of the tiny windows.

Mac stood on the porch.

I opened the door.

As alluring as I looked in the baggy outfit with fuzzy leopard-print slippers on my feet, he didn't take my appearance in my pajamas as an invitation. My mother would have fainted at the idea that I was letting a man see me in my sleepwear.

"I thought you were through questioning me." I hugged myself to keep warm in the chilly air from the open door.

"Well, after I talked to the kids, I thought you might clarify a few things for me."

"Come in, then. Would you like something hot to drink? I don't have anything but instant coffee. Or you could have a mug of what I'm having." I stepped back and let him in, then led him into the kitchen. Gus looked at him briefly, then back to me. Deciding that I could not offer him my full attention, the cat declined to follow us and chose to pile up on the couch in the living room.

"You got any of those little marshmallows?" His face was solemn enough for me to believe the answer might matter, but his tone was teasing. I matched it with my response.

"You betcha. Come on out to the kitchen."

Mac followed me into the tiny room and sat down at the chrome dinette table that just fit in one corner. He wasn't a big man, but he filled the space with an air of competence. He wore neatly pressed jeans, a plaid flannel shirt, and what I'd always thought of as a "vanity belt." Big belt buckle and his name stenciled on the back. When I was in college in Durant, the joke was that a cowboy wore a belt like that so he wouldn't forget his name. But Mac didn't have the hat to go with the rest of the ensemble, and his hair was a little longer than most cowboys, the dark wings of it covering the tops of his ears and brushing his collar.

"You didn't tell me Chris's dad made him quit the play."

"Yes. That had just come up yesterday." I had to talk over my shoulder as I filled the kettle and set it on the stove to heat.

"The boy wasn't very happy about it."

"No."

"Was he unhappy enough to murder?"

I sat down at the table. "Chris? A murderer? No, I don't think so. He was quite calm when he came to tell me he had to quit. I've always known him to do exactly what his father wanted him to do. It would be difficult to do otherwise. Colonel Slayton is ... was ... a very overbearing person."

"Was that your experience with him?"

"Well, we had never really crossed paths before Chris became involved in the play."

Mac raised his eyebrows at that. "Quanah is a small school. I'd think the teachers would know each other real well."

"Some of us do." I tried staring down into the hot chocolate in front of me to keep from staring into Mac's eyes, eyes almost the same hazelnut color of the hot chocolate. Keeping Mac from suspecting how I felt about him was going to be difficult. The feeling ... raw attraction ... was simple. I tilted my head up to finish my thought.

"You have to understand that, at Quanah, being on the faculty is sort of like being in high school yourself. There are 'cliques' among teachers as well as the students. The men hang together, and the women hang together."

"Who do you hang with?"

"Lenore Roland, mostly."

"And the colonel?"

"I guess Garrett, one of our science teachers, more than anyone. The two of them were practically the only men in the high school who weren't coaches as well as teachers."

"Did Slayton and Garrett have something else in common that made them friendly?"

"They both have a military background. That's about it." The kettle whistled, so I stood and mixed a mug of hot chocolate for Mac, setting it down in front of him and offering a bag of mini-marshmallows.

"It's better if you put the marshmallows in before you pour the hot water over it." He stirred the little white pellets into the chocolate so they would melt and then continued, "Sort that out for me ... why 'Colonel' Slayton?"

"He's an ex-Marine."

"How did he end up in Quanah?"

"I think he's part of that Troops to Teachers program." I watched Mac raise his eyebrows as he sipped his hot chocolate, signaling me to go on. "Retired military personnel can get their teaching certificate on a fast track and go to work in the classroom. I don't know why he ended up in Quanah specifically. I haven't heard about any family connection."

"What kind of teacher is he?"

"Math."

"I mean, how good is he?"

"I don't know firsthand. I've only heard from students what the colonel's classes were like." I didn't want to bad-mouth a fellow teacher, especially one who was dead. If Mac pressed me for details about Slayton's classroom demeanor, I couldn't stay positive.

"And that was?"

"Very regimented. Almost militaristic." Mac's eyes widened. "Look, it's not like we go nuts in my classroom, but I happen to believe that my students are young adults, and they have to make choices about their behavior. The only choice Slayton gave kids was 'my way or the highway.'"

"My point exactly. Don't you think there's bound to be one time when the pressure to do what Daddy wants is finally too much?" Mac didn't have his notebook out, but his focus on me as I answered his questions told me he didn't need to write down every detail.

"You're the sheriff. I'm just the teacher who saw Chris every single day of his senior year. And I'm telling you, he wasn't that kind of boy." I didn't want Mac to ignore my perspective. "You've put me in a bad position, showing up at my door at midnight to ask me these questions. The least you can do is listen to what I have to say."

"You didn't have to let me in the door." Pointing out the obvious, Mac shut me up for a second.

"You asked me if the pressure on Chris was enough to make him kill his own father."

"It's a motive."

"I'll tell you again. Chris wasn't out of my sight during rehearsal. He was on stage or on the front row."

"You admitted the colonel managed to slip backstage without you noticing. And Libby left the building without drawing your attention." His calm recitation of facts wasn't a question, but his list did seem to lead to the conclusion that Chris might have been able to sneak away.

"I understand what you're trying to say, but my focus was on the actors. We were working. Chris was either onstage reading Romeo's lines or in the front row helping Adam read them."

Mac stared at me, his eyes piercing me with rapt attention. It wasn't a man/woman thing, but I couldn't help imagining what it would be like if it were.

"I haven't talked to Libby yet. She wasn't at home when I swung by a little while ago."

"She probably doesn't even know what's happened if she hasn't got a message from the faculty phone tree." I looked down into the almost empty cup and thought for a second. "Libby's pretty unconventional."

Mac was good with silences. When he wanted me to explain something, he just looked at me until I started talking again.

"I mean Libby is at the opposite end of the spectrum from Slayton. And it has always shown."

"Some kind of conflict there?"

"They were neighbors. On the hallway at school, I mean. The history classes are right next door to the math classes, and I think Slayton thought Libby was disruptive."

"And was she?"

"Not to me." I thought I should stop before I gave him a reason to really suspect Libby. Yes, her classes were boisterous. Her goal was to help students experience history. Her history classroom was rich with conversation and music from whatever era she and her students were discussing. Definitely not in tune with Slayton's pedagogy.

Was a difference in teaching style enough motive for murder?

Mac drank the last of the hot chocolate, and then stood up, wiping his mouth with the back of his hand. "Thanks for the chocolate. Feels real good on a cold night. Oh, one more thing. Apparently, someone stabbed the colonel."

"Stabbed?"

"With a real pretty knife. About yay long," he held his hands about a foot apart, "and covered with fake jewels. Does that ring a bell?"

A sick lump in my stomach bobbed, and my nervous system went into little spasms. On my mind's screen, I saw the black and white "Please Stand By. We're Having Technical Difficulties" sign. All the worrying about a connection between the colonel's misadventure and the cast and crew of my play popped back up to the surface. I tried to keep my voice calm as I answered Mac.

"Yes, that's a dagger Libby Hoffman gave me to use in the play. She'd got it from a friend who'd found it in Venice or somewhere. I gave it to Rick to lock away until it was time for Juliet to brandish it around."

Rick handled the prop last. He'd stowed it during rehearsal the day before, and we hadn't needed to bring it out tonight. Rick didn't have any reason to harm the colonel. Did he?

Rick was in the colonel's algebra class. He must have had a passing grade. If he wasn't, he would have been on the list of students who were making "F"s, and I wouldn't have been able to use him as stage manager. Again, I wondered if petty matters like grades were motive enough for murder. I couldn't imagine what would motivate me to commit homicide, and I winced at the times I'd said, "I want to kill those kids."

"If I have anything else to ask, I'll be in touch." Mac headed toward the front door.

"Yes. Be sure to be in touch." This time when he fixed his gaze on me, it was a man/woman thing. I thought about Scarlett saying that every time Rhett Butler looked at her, she felt like he could see her in her shimmy. Maybe next time I opened the door for Mac I should be wearing more.

Or less.

CHAPTER SIX

The crowd between my parking space and the front door of the school almost kept me from parking at all when I arrived Friday morning. I nosed my little black Mini Cooper through the crush of reporters and around the satellite trucks to park in the space marked with my name. Shouldering my bag of papers, I got out and tried to judge whether there was a way to get in the front door without crossing in front of a camera.

The reporter from Channel 8 stood in front of the building where metal letters across the red brick spelled out Quanah High School. Her brown suit was a shade slightly too dark to blend with the bricks behind the silver letters. Channel 6's reporter had staked out the real estate in front of the glass doors leading into the lobby where we'd gathered last night.

I dodged the Channel 6 crew and slipped behind the bunch from the other station, opening the front door with Lenore right behind me. We headed straight for the library and the faculty meeting Bart Lincoln had called.

"I saw some of the coverage this morning over breakfast," Lenore told me. "Quanah makes the television news about twice a year. Once in the fall, when they fly by one of the football games on a Friday night, and then when someone dies."

"You make it sound like murder is an annual event."

"I just meant Quanah's never in the news except when something terrible happens. Why can't they bring in the cameras for Pioneer Days, or when the Chamber of Commerce cuts a ribbon on a new business?" Lenore wasn't given to rants, but she embellished her argument. "When Jud Wilson had a tomato that looked just like Marilyn Monroe, no one came out to film that."

"A voluptuous tomato is front-page news for our paper here in town, but good news is no news in the big city. You don't really think Jud's tomato deserved a live remote, do you?"

"The other night I saw them talking about some people who had helped a man gather up his money after a stiff wind got it at the ATM. You can't call that news."

"I saw that too. Some town in California. The weird coast. Quanah is to Tulsa what the Midwest is to the East and West coasts ... largely invisible." I nodded to students as we made our way to the library.

When we opened the double doors to the library, we found most of the high school teachers

47

already seated at the round tables scattered around the room. At a regular faculty meeting, someone would have commented on how quickly the donuts disappeared once the coaches showed up from the morning bus routes. This morning, I heard only low voices and none of the good-natured teasing that usually went back and forth between OU and OSU fans.

There weren't even any donuts this morning.

Lenore and I sat with the other two English teachers at a table near the back of the room. ~~Libby sat down at the table behind us just before~~ Bart Lincoln entered the library and stood behind the checkout desk. He stared at a legal pad. I doubted his hesitancy to begin had anything to do with a surfeit of emotion about the colonel. The principal had a lot to explain, starting with why a teacher wasn't safe in our own school.

"~~Mr. Johnson wanted us to meet as a district~~ faculty, but I thought it would be better if we talked as a high school family first," he began.

I tried not to roll my eyes. He had a tough crowd and an awful situation to deal with in the aftermath of the colonel's death. The faculty seated in the library was only part of the problem. The superintendent, Walter Johnson, could support Bart when parents started calling for his hide, or he could use Bart as a shield between him and the publicity ~~mill grinding out front.~~

"We've lost one of our family," Bart ~~continued~~ said. ~~I heard Libby snort and turned to her. Her face was blank. I turned back to listen to the rest of what Bart had to say.~~ "The colonel will be missed, I know.

Ginny has told us the funeral is Saturday at the Baptist church ... that's the Grace Baptist, here in town. We'll be sending flowers from the faculty."

"Bart, why are we here today? Are we safe?" Our Family and Consumer Science teacher had broken in without raising her hand. No one objected. We all wanted answers to the same questions.

"Well, Helen, we're here for the kids."

The school day wouldn't be like any other Friday, but we would try to make it as normal as possible. The effort was good for the kids. Students with a strong connection to the colonel, or to Chris, would need the structure to help hold themselves together. Other students needed to stay occupied so they didn't fall prey to the rumor mill or start mischief out on their own. Even in the few years I'd been at Quanah, I'd learned how a school could best handle a tragedy: together. Dealing with the death of a student or a colleague isn't one of the topics they cover in education programs, but both were realities every teacher in the building had faced. To outsiders, it seemed cold-blooded to have school when one of our own was dead. To us, it was a chance to support and look out for one another.

Bart said, "We're safe. Our Sheriff is investigating, and we are keeping a close eye on everything today. Mac has sent Deputy Standfield down to patrol the halls, and he and my second in command, Millard, are out and about as the kids are coming in this morning."

When Bart finished speaking, our counselor, Linda Savitch, explained how she had teamed up with the junior high and elementary counselors to work with students who might need them.

"Y'all," Linda said, trying to get our attention, "Y'all, these kids may not register what they are really experiencing. Even if the colonel wasn't one of their favorite teachers, the fact of his death happening so close here is bound to affect them."

I couldn't predict how Slayton's death would affect his popularity. Sometimes when a student died, his or her popularity soared in the aftermath. Everyone had been his best friend. She had said something special to each person the day before it happened. But when a teacher passed away, how would the students react?

"If you see a kid acting suspiciously, if they're tensed up or more volatile than usual, send someone with them to come see me." Linda had handouts on the grieving process to share with us and moved around the room to distribute them.

Bart took the floor again before he sent us to class. "If you hear anything, it's your responsibility to let us know. Anything. This is not a joking matter. A kid that spouts off about this, well, he might be the kid that did it. So watch 'em."

Lenore and I both rolled our eyes. Teenagers used tasteless jokes to deal with highly emotional events. Jokes about OJ Simpson floated around when I was in high school. I didn't laugh at those, and I knew I wouldn't laugh at jokes about the colonel's nasty end, but I also knew a joke wasn't a confession.

Libby rushed out of the library before we could speak to her, and the rest of the faculty left for their rooms. Stephen Keener stopped to talk to Bart. I grimaced. I'd forgotten to tell Mae about the coach's presence at rehearsal yesterday. He'd want to know.

Tight little groups of kids holding on to each other like bobbing life rafts crowded the hallways as Lenore and I worked our way to our classrooms. As soon as I sat down, I tried to compose an e-mail to some parents about a plagiarism problem in first hour. Writing the note was such an ordinary act that I felt a little ashamed.

Every time my fingers paused above the keyboard, a fuzzy picture formed: Slayton prone on the floor, and the blood spreading on the concrete.

I tried to focus on the e-mails, but then I started to think about how close the students and I had been to death the night before. What would have happened if one of the students had gone backstage and found the colonel and his attacker struggling?

I kept tapping at the keys, pushing the pictures away and purposely musing about how e-mail changed my life as a teacher. I didn't like to admit how e-mail shielded me from conflicts that might arise in conversations on the phone or face-to-face with parents. I liked to rehearse conversations I thought might get heated. Parents often reacted strongly when they were blindsided with a misdeed I attributed to their son or daughter.

"Mrs. Lummox, I found a can in my room that little Rowdy has been using as a spit cup for his chewing tobacco habit," I'd begin. Teachers should offer something positive before getting down to the problem so parents wouldn't be defensive. However, sometimes positive wasn't possible, so I chose factual.

"Rowdy doesn't chew tobacco. It has to be some other student," the parent would reply.

"No, I took the can from Rowdy's own hand, and he signed the detention slip. I wanted you to know because I'm sure you'll want to act on such information." The last few words were meant to be a bonding statement, to assure Mrs. Lummox we were in this adventure in adolescent land together.

Sometimes it worked.

"I will sue the hell out of you and anyone else in that school if you continue to harass my son! I'll be talking to the superintendent about your attitude!"

Sometimes it didn't.

I stopped typing. Writing one e-mail for the half-dozen plagiarists and sending it to a list of recipients wouldn't do. The contact had to be personal. I'd have to speak to the parents so I could emphasize the seriousness of the incident.

I closed my e-mail and opened up the online attendance program we used to look up phone numbers.

I'd start with Abby's parents. Her mom, Jessica, was one of those pillars of the school who was always pitching in and was super supportive of teachers and school activities. In fact, Mrs. Beamer piloted the local chapter of Moms in Touch. The group met weekly to pray for the teachers in our district. Jessica and I would chat about Abby's faux pas, and then with a little success under my belt, I could move on to other, less genial, parents. I wrote down the numbers I needed, trying to keep rehearsing what I would say to the parents instead of picturing the scene backstage last night.

While my room was still empty, I picked up the phone and dialed the Beamers' number. Abby's mom picked up on the second ring, answering with a breathless, "Hello?"

"Mrs. Beamer? Regina Murphy, Abby's drama teacher."

"Oh, how nice! How is everyone holding up there?"

"It's a strange day, but I think things are under control."

"I've got to tell you, the most awful stories are going around. That colonel was into some rather unsavory things, I hear." Mrs. Beamer's voice went up in pitch at the end, making her statement into a question to which I had no answer.

"I'm unaware of anything like that. The sheriff is on the case now." And would not appreciate Mrs. Beamer's appetite for dirt. Or would Mac want to know what people were saying? I decided I might need to tell him, but first I tried to steer Mrs. Beamer back to the purpose of my call. "I'm calling about something else, Mrs. Beamer—"

"Jessica, please! We've worked on enough fundraisers together to be on a first-name basis, don't you think?"

"Well, of course we have! I'm calling about a problem I'm having with Abby."

"Oh, dear. I'm sure nothing too bad has happened? Our Abby is quite the conscientious girl."

"Well, yes, she has always been a pleasure to work with, but we need to discuss a problem with her latest drama assignment. She turned in work that was not her own. She plagiarized a large part of her latest essay."

A slight rustle told me she was making a gesture I'd seen her use when she was concentrating: as she rapidly nodded her head in affirmation that she had heard, her lips would pucker into a drawstring of confusion.

Finally, she spoke. "You mean she copied someone else's work?"

"She took material from the Internet and used it instead of writing her own essay."

"I see. Well, plagiarism is not acceptable." Jessica's response reassured me. "How will you be dealing with this?"

"I've given her a zero for the assignment."

Another rustle as she took in my response.

"And how will she make up this zero? How will she keep her "A" in your class?"

"She won't make up the assignment she plagiarized since she chose not to complete the essay herself. Her grade will dip a bit, but it should rise again as she completes the work for the semester. She can still earn an "A"."

"Yes, I see." A long pause. Another rustle. "Her father and I will talk to her as well. Thank you so much for calling!"

Once the conversation was over, I felt as though my shoulders were bunched up beside my ears. I shrugged, trying to loosen the muscles. I'd informed Abby's mom, she hadn't yelled at me or called me names or threatened to whip Abby upon her return home. She hadn't threatened to sue me, Bart, or the district.

I was starting the day with a win.

CHAPTER SEVEN

I kept the temperature in my room on the edge of chilly because a little cold helped keep the students focused. No one in my first-hour English class fell asleep, even when I'd tried to lead a conversation about dangling modifiers. The energy drinks they'd gulped down on their way into class kept them from zoning out while I explained why *'the woman hanging in the tree found the balloon'* was not interchangeable with *'the woman found the balloon hanging in the tree'*.

I glanced at the clock. Only a few minutes of class remained. "I'll have your papers back tomorrow. When the bell rings, I need to see Abby at my desk."

Students turned to each other to chat for the last few minutes of class, and I tried to organize the drift of papers on my desk with Abby's assignment on top.

When the bell sounded and the rest of the students crowded out of the classroom, Abby approached me. Her physical presence reflected my own inner tension as she alternately tensed and relaxed. Her hands kneaded her upper arms as she stood in front of my desk. Her face first crumpled and then smoothed out, like a piece of paper discarded and then reconsidered.

She knew why I had asked her to stay.

"That paper was my original work, Ms. Murphy!"

"Stop there. It was not. This is what I printed off the web." I handed her the stapled papers. "You cut and pasted and turned the result in for a grade."

Abby's head bowed over the papers. In the still classroom, the ticking of the clock was magnified.

"You said we should do some research."

"Yes. But when you research, you think about what the sources say and put the ideas in your own words." I paused again.

She spoke sooner this time.

"You just don't like me; you've had it in for me all semester. If you liked me, I'd be playing Juliet!" Abby's shoulders straightened and she tilted her chin up, defying me to disagree with her.

"Abby, you're doing a wonderful job as the nurse. Your best contribution to the play is to keep playing her as well as you have been." I sighed at her complete lack of insight into her own talents. Her sense of comic timing was better than any other girl who'd read for the part. More than that, she had nurse energy. I could imagine her taking Romeo or Benvolio by the ear if they sassed her. "We're not talking about the play. We need to talk about why you chose to cheat on this assignment."

"I've got too much to do. I gave up starting in basketball so I can make play rehearsal, and soccer starts soon. Everyone wants something from me and I can't make everyone happy." She wilted a little, as if the weight of everyone's expectations was a literal burden instead of a psychological weight.

"So who's unhappy now? You can't make anyone who cares about you happy if you're not happy with yourself." I moved around the desk and sat on its edge. "You've got a zero for this assignment. Your grade will dip, but because it's still early in the semester you can recover. But you've got to make some choices about how to manage your time. You're trying to do too much."

"You want me to quit the play!"

"No, I want you to do what's best for you. I want you to stay in the play."

"My parents won't let me quit basketball. And they're going to freak when I bring home this "F"." Abby's demeanor shifted once again, revealing the very reason I thought she was a good actress; her ability to convey emotions physically made her a natural for the stage. She said, "They already raked me and Colonel Slayton over the coals because of my geometry grade."

I was surprised, not that she'd been having problems in Geometry, but that her parents had had a conflict with the colonel. Her mom had seemed so reasonable when we spoke on the phone.

Abby's expression changed again. Without looking at me she said, "We could keep it between us. You know I'll never pull this again."

"Yes. But your parents have to know. What if they get your midterm grade and wonder what happened? Then they'd be upset you'd kept it from them."

And upset with me for keeping them out of the loop.

"That would be worse."

"It would be. I've already talked to your mom. There's no putting that cat back in the bag. Now, scat. I'm not writing you a note if you're late to next hour. See you at rehearsal."

CHAPTER EIGHT

In the hour and a half since I'd walked through the door at a quarter to eight, I'd been questioned by several students about what had really happened at rehearsal on Thursday. Some asked, "Are you doing okay?"

"Okay" was relative. I felt safe in the halls and classroom, but a level of anxiety at the thought of returning to the auditorium for rehearsal hummed in my subconscious. After the attack on the colonel, I was hyperaware of how I might keep the students safe from intruders.

The questions kept coming as students entered my room for third period. "Ms. Murphy, is it true Chris's dad was a CIA agent and the government had to have him killed because he was ready to talk?" The freshman girl, pink as bubblegum and just as bright, leaned over my desk, her eyebrows stretched nearly to her hairline.

I pushed my own hair back behind my ears in an unconscious effort to rearrange hers before I answered.

"No, Brenda, I doubt that story is true. You have to be careful about saying things like that where people can hear. You might start a rumor." She just rolled her eyes and joined the other students settling into desks. The rumor mill ground very fast at Quanah High School, but you couldn't always tell what the end product would be.

Students hadn't learned not to ask difficult questions. One had asked me if I'd committed the murder because the colonel wouldn't respond to my feminine wiles. That's the genteel translation of his question. What he actually said was "Ms. Murphy, did you do in the colonel because he wouldn't give you any?" I referred him to Mr. Lincoln for discipline.

Stacie Linheart had confided to her neighbor in my first-hour class that she and Chris had been planning to go to "Elm Tree" Friday and that his father had opposed the relationship because her parents were anti-war protesters "back in the day."

I believed the colonel would object to Chris dating the girl, who constantly carried "sweet savage" paperbacks in her backpack and dragged them out to read anytime we had a few minutes in class. I'd glance up from grading a paper, or turn around from the board to call on someone, and be confronted by a male with a better chest than me bending an even more buxom damsel backwards over the torrid script of the latest title. I did not believe Chris had plans to date Stacie. I also did not believe that Chris planned to take her to the notorious make out spot at the lake, since he didn't have a car of his own yet.

I'd even heard that Chris murdered his dad because the colonel didn't want him to be in the play. The rumor of patricide was uncomfortably close to my own initial analysis of the situation, but since I wasn't a trained detective, I thought it would be best if I kept my opinions about the identity of the murderer to myself. I didn't know Chris as well as I knew most of my other students, but he appeared to have been grieving for his father when I talked to him Saturday. Even Chris, who was a talented high school actor, couldn't fake the emotion I saw in him the day before. But what emotion did I see? He could have been grieving. Or he could have been remorseful. I'd told Mac I knew Chris well enough that he shouldn't be a suspect. What if I was wrong?

"Please take a seat, Lab," I asked my Mercutio when I saw him loitering by the lunch menu after the bell rang.

"Where do you want me to take it?"

"The originality of that line is stunning. I've taught ten years, and I've only heard it once a week since I was twenty-five. Put *your* seat in *that* seat and catch up."

I made a few notes on the board and then handed out a worksheet on changes in Renaissance stage design. While students worked, I retired behind my desk and flipped through the costume book Libby had given me. The text looked Italian, but the pictures spoke to me.

Even in the rather crude sketches and woodcuts reproduced in the book, the clothing looked sumptuous. I wanted to recreate these clothes for our play. But how do you get the look of careless glamour on our limited budget? I remembered once seeing some costumes constructed largely of upholstery fabric at a Renaissance Fair. One year I'd directed *The Taming of the Shrew* for our fall play, and we still had a dress a volunteer had built for us, the base of which was a velour bathrobe from Sears. From the audience, the robe looked the part of a sweeping velvet gown. We could create some beautiful, believable costumes out of not much more than a trip to a thrift store and a glue gun. I flipped back to the front of the book to check the table of contents for a resource section.

A loud bang, the unmistakable sound of a body hitting a locker, startled me, and I moved to investigate even as I gave my class the "stay where you are or you'll get hurt" look. Even before I made it out into the hall, I could hear Chris yelling.

"I don't know what you think I did, but I didn't have anything to do with it."

I saw Shrimp, half-hidden behind Chris's lanky frame as they wrestled against the row of lockers directly across from my room. If I'd turned around, I knew I would have found twenty-three faces pressed up against the floor-to-ceiling window behind me. I chose not to give into the temptation, but I felt 46 eyes boring into my back. I planted my feet and spoke.

"Shrimp!"

He ignored me, still trying to subdue Chris. Shrimp's handcuffs flopped loosely. He struggled to capture Chris's wrists.

"Shrimp Stanfield, this is a school. Students are supposed to be learning. What do you think you're doing?" My tone made him pause and blink at me. Before the deputy could open his mouth to explain, Bart Lincoln appeared from a classroom just to the right of the lockers.

"I assure you, Ms. Murphy, we have everything under control." Bart's nervous tug at his tie didn't inspire any confidence. "I was trying to inspect the colonel's classroom and found this one in there, playing hooky."

"And so you tackled him?" I glared at the deputy.

"He ran," Shrimp shrugged.

"What are you doing here, Chris? You should be home with your mom."

"I had to get out of the house, and it just felt safer to come here. All my friends are here. Then this cracker," Chris nodded back at Shrimp, "says he's taking me in for questioning. They think I killed my dad!"

"I've got plenty of reasons to haul you in," Shrimp said. "Your backpack has several cans of spray paint in it, and I can't think of a good reason that'd be. And you left your momma at home by herself to come up here."

"None of that means I killed my Dad."

"None of it means you didn't, either."

Chris snorted, but quit struggling. The deputy put the handcuffs around his wrists. The boy's shoulders slumped, and his pale face looked clammy under his limp hair.

"We wouldn't have this problem if you'd of just come with me nice and talked to us," Shrimp said.

The deputy pulled up on the cuffs holding Chris's hands behind his back. Chris yelped like a puppy. Shrimp dragged him away from the classrooms toward the front entrance. My instinct made me take a step with him, but I stopped myself from getting closer. I didn't want to give Shrimp any reason to overreact.

Bart spoke. "Chris. Mr. Standfield. We do have this situation under control. Ms. Murphy, return to your room. Your students appear concerned about your whereabouts. See me in my office on your planning period."

Lincoln's stiff manner betrayed his annoyance with how Shrimp had apprehended Chris. Disturbances of any kind were not welcome. If he had called me in to discuss the boisterousness of my class when we had a good day reading the Scottish play (witches were loud, the kids had maintained), then I could only imagine how an altercation with law enforcement in his hallway tilted his universe.

"Of course, Mr. Lincoln. I was concerned the incident was a threat to a student." I tried not to look irritated, but Lincoln should have known Shrimp was likely to make a scene when he came in looking for Chris.

Shrimp was a small man with a big ego. When we'd gone to the chamber's Christmas banquet, he'd told me he had to carry his service revolver all the time and I shouldn't be surprised if I felt something hard when I snuggled up to him. Entering the school cafeteria for the dinner, Shrimp kept my hand clamped in his and headed straight for the chamber president's table where he assured Leon that the venue was safe, and Shrimp was there to keep it so.

Lincoln's directive had been his exit line, so I turned back to see my students scattering to their desks. I shut the door behind me when I entered the class.

After seeing Chris handcuffed and dragged away, I couldn't pretend that Renaissance stagecraft mattered. We could still hear scuffling, the hollow thump of a body colliding with a locker, Shrimp's Barney Fife pitch grumbling as he tried to keep Chris subdued, and Lincoln's voice, deep enough to carry authority, but not meaning, through the wall.

I sat on the high plastic chair behind my podium. I tapped my pencil on the wood. I crossed my legs and swung one foot, admiring the neat pair of brick red pumps I'd put on that morning. The students stared at me. The silence frightened me a little. I had never heard the classroom so still. Not even when I was in the middle of my passionate explanation of the theater of the absurd in the spring. The quiet reminded me of a cliché: "be careful what you wish for; you might get it." Here was what I had thought I dreamed of: a class of teenagers with every mouth closed, every cell phone stilled, every digit frozen and non-texting, every eye directed at me.

And I had nothing.

"So, how about those Italians? Gave up theater for opera, huh?" I said.

Even Lab frowned at me and my lame effort to reengage the class.

"Look, I know he's your friend. What would you say to him if you could talk to him right now?" I dropped the pencil on the podium and leaned forward.

"It's not that far to the Mexican border!" Lab's desperate humor earned him muffled laughter from his classmates.

"Yeah, Lab. You tell 'em," one of the approval-seeking sophomores called out. "Ask him what flavor of cake does he want around his file."

Lab froze him with an arched eyebrow and a studied sneer. "That was totally gay. You don't know Chris. You're not even an upperclassman. We know it's all good. Chris wouldn't hurt his dad, no matter what a dick he was."

"Language!"

Lab snorted. "Language? Shrimp just hauled off your boy. What's a four-letter word when Chris is chillin' in jail?"

I nodded.

The exchange thawed the class enough that we might be able to do something productive. Oh, the changes in technical theater weren't going to recapture anyone's interest, including mine. But they all seemed interested in what they could do for Chris. None of them expressed, even in guarded looks, the idea that Chris might really have murdered his father.

The realization that none of them suspected Chris comforted me. One thing I had learned as a teacher: kids know. They knew stuff about their peers, who was into drugs and what kind and who was crushed out on whom. But they knew the big stuff too. Or what passed for big stuff in adult world. They knew what teacher was going to resign at the next board meeting before it made the board's agenda. They knew what teachers drank and where.

They knew, somehow, that Chris was not a murderer. So I knew it, too.
How would Mac know?

CHAPTER NINE

Since I'd become a teacher, visiting the principal's office was easier than it had been when I was a student, twenty years ago, but not by much. I still felt a flat, rolling plate inside my stomach at the thought of sitting down with Bart. I dawdled at the mailboxes in the reception area on my way to see him. Most of my mail I tossed into the trash without opening.

The office was usually calm, with a student aide sitting behind the front counter, looking through an issue of *People* and waiting for the phone to ring. Today, the aide's magazine lay abandoned as she answered call after call, transferring some and taking messages for others. Several people I recognized from standups on the evening news sat in chairs against the wall opposite the counter, each of them displaying unique markers of impatience. One woman's foot tapped out the "William Tell Overture" as she scrolled through messages on her phone. A man in a rumpled suit, too rumpled for TV, I thought, sat with his legs stretched out and kept trying to take a sip of water from an empty bottle. Another man sat up straight in the chair, as tense as a racehorse in the starting gate.

Carolyn, our receptionist, stood at the counter flipping through the transcript book. Carolyn was at the center of the complex social universe of Quanah. She had an encyclopedic memory in which she stored the relationships among students at Quanah High School past and present as well as the local phone directory. You didn't need a phone book if you could ask Carolyn, and you didn't need a telephone to spread the word. Just tell Carolyn.

I raised eyebrows and tilted my head toward the gallery of strangers.

She shrugged. "They're waiting to talk to Bart."

"Isn't he with the superintendent?"

"Yes, I've told them Bart isn't available, but they seem to think he'll be available. Or they'll ambush him on his way to lunch." When she shook her head at their cluelessness, her hair bobbed back and forth, emphasizing her gesture. Carolyn visited Tawnette's House of Beauty every Thursday after school, and the resulting confection that sat on top of her head looked as though someone had wrapped yarn around a projecting spindle and then fluffed it. Without the pert nose and sharp chin, she would have looked like a troll doll whose hair had escaped the vat of dye.

I thought about the likelihood of offering Carolyn and Libby up as makeover candidates if Tim Gunn were ever to show up in Quanah. I'd submit myself too. At the end of the show, Carolyn would have a smooth waterfall of hair falling in a casual bob, Libby would be wearing jewel tones instead of earth tones, and I would be sporting a swingy skirt and sweater set rather than the ubiquitous pantsuit.

Fantasy over, I watched Carolyn pull a pencil out from behind her ear and check off a name on the list beside the binder in front of her. Her movements reminded me of the t'ai chi practitioners on the local university's television channel.

"Bart's not in his office, is he?"

"Yeah, he's there," Carolyn confirmed.

Damn.

"Shrimp and the sheriff went on their way, and Bart's been in his little cave ever since."

"Do you think they'll keep Chris? I don't really think he did it, but I don't know how the wheels of justice work in this town."

"And where were you living during the last election?"

"Well, here, but I've never paid attention to local crime. I've never had to."

"The wheels of justice turn just fine since Mac's been sheriff. That's why you haven't had to think about it. I imagine he'll be real quick to find out Chris didn't have anything to do with his daddy's death." Carolyn was firm. "He can only hold him so long, anyway. He could just give him a good talking to and release him to his mom, but if Mac thinks Chris has anything to do with the colonel's murder, he's going to have to refer him to the juvenile court."

Like I said, her knowledge was encyclopedic.

"Chris is a pretty sensitive boy. I hate to think of him behind bars."

"Have you seen the set up they've got at the jail, Reg? The last sheriff's wife made curtains for the jail cell window. It's not McAlester down there."

"Well, that's a little bit of a relief."

Down the hall, I tapped on Bart's open door before entering. He turned to me, away from his computer, and motioned me to sit down.

"Ms. Murphy, I want us to have a little talk." Bart could only metaphorically roll up his sleeves, as he wore a tan, short-sleeved dress shirt. He also wore a clip-on tie with stripes of our school colors, blue and gold. I tried not to sneer at his fashion choices as he continued.

"The Beamers gave me a little visit yesterday about you and Abby."

"Yes, I've talked to Mrs. Beamer. She was very nice." The disc in my stomach settled like a hula hoop rolling to a stop.

"They're not happy that you've come down on their little girl so hard over such a minor matter." Bart leaned forward, his hands clasped on the desk pad before him. He tried to look nonthreatening, but his eyes narrowed as though he was sighting down a rifle and I was the deer at the other end. He'd caught me now. I'd made the Beamers unhappy. Given their stature in our town, the Beamers were like Dr. Phil's momma: If they ain't happy, ain't nobody happy.

"I don't feel the incident was minor. She copied a paper off the Internet and turned it in as her own work."

"Now, you know sometimes our students are under a lot of pressure and they look for ways to make life easier for themselves." He flexed his hands open as if to welcome me into the fold with this interpretation. I was not ready to be herded. "And Abby, she's one of our best and brightest. Her folks are set on her going to one of those Ivy League schools after she leaves here and this mark on her record could put the kibosh on that."

"I'm sure the pressure from her parents may explain why she plagiarized the work, but it certainly doesn't excuse her choice to cheat."

"Sometimes, we have to give kids room to make a mistake. Now, Abby is a good girl. She's right there at the top of her class, and I'd hate to see a little misunderstanding ruin that honor for her."

"Abby understood me perfectly when I told her what she did was wrong. She was contrite about the whole episode. I understand now why she didn't want me to tell her parents. She was afraid of something like this happening!"

"Something like what, Ms. Murphy?"

"Something like a pissant principal making excuses for her." My hand flew to cover my mouth, and I opened my eyes wide in shock at my word choice. Oh god, oh god, oh god ... I did so like my job, and I'd hate to move on, but it looked like I'd be doing just that.

Bart continued as if I hadn't spoken at all. "Something like an administrator trying to rein you in before you cause any more damage? We've talked before. You need to get with the program and make sure you're not holding back our best kids.

You're going to ruin her reputation before she can move on and achieve all the stuff we know she's capable of."

"Unless you and her parents try to make an issue out of it, Bart, no one is going to know anything to tarnish her reputation. I talked to her privately. I took into consideration her usual standards of behavior—excellent—as well as her choice this time—poor. If her parents want to stir it up, they need to know that trying to blacken my reputation will blacken their daughter's as well."

"You aren't threatening the Beamers, are you, Reg? They're not the ones we need to be concerned with. You are. When we talked about your choice of spring play last year, I told you I had my eye on you and if you got off track there'd be consequences."

"I'm not threatening anyone. I'm just pointing out that they can't make a big stink and keep Abby smelling like a rose." My hands had balled into fists, and my throat tightened until my voice squeaked. I took a deep breath and intentionally relaxed my hands. "Abby is a very talented girl, and I thought after we'd talked, she was ready to make the right decision."

"Reg, the Beamers had been in to talk to me about the colonel's classroom just week before last. I stood up for him, you know. I explained how a teacher can run his classroom any way he sees fit, although I think we should all subscribe to that hypocritic oath."

"The hypocritic oath?"

"First, do no harm."

The Hippocratic Oath. Got it.

"The Beamers felt like the colonel wasn't treating Abby fairly," Bart said.

I'd been cursed out and called unrepeatable names by parents, but I'd never been directly threatened. Quanah just wasn't that kind of town. Until now.

Bart's words penetrated my musings, as he said, "But, Reg, the Beamers are a little more put out with you."

They'd been put out with the colonel, and now he was dead. What would push a couple so venerated for their community work to murder someone? Parents might have issues with an English teacher for teaching a book they felt was inappropriate. Lenore had to defend *Brave New World* one year when a few parents objected. Our science teacher walked a tightrope in even mentioning evolution in biology. Coaches were frequently targeted because they made some students ride the bench or cut someone from the team.

Unless Abby had been taking shortcuts in Slayton's class like she had in mine, I couldn't think of anything the Beamers might be upset about.

"What problem did the Beamers have with the colonel?"

"Now, Reg, I can't speak to that. I'd hate to speak ill of the dead, you know."

"You just told me yourself you'd stood up for him, so it couldn't have been a big deal. The Beamers have been here a lot longer than the colonel, and I'm sure you'd rush to smooth it over with them before you'd protect us." Today was my day for being frank. I'd thrown caution to the wind, and Bart's color deepened. I'd hit a nerve.

"Reg, what went on between the Beamers and me is absolutely confidential. What we're here to discuss is how you've mishandled this whole thing with Abby."

"Have you talked to Abby?"

The lines on Bart's face fell away as his eyes widened in confusion. "Abby?"

"Yes, Abby, the girl at the center of the incident we're discussing."

"No. Her parents and I are handling it."

"I think you need to check in with Abby before we go any farther. She was terrified her parents would find out about her plagiarism, and now I know why. She's a sensible girl. She knew she should have done the work herself. She was afraid her parents would come up here and make another scene, which they have." I was repeating myself, but Bart hadn't heard me the first time.

"Reg, don't think you've scored any points here today. You're young and you can afford to float on to another job if this one doesn't work out."

"Bart, one of the wisest things Lenore has ever said to me is that teachers outlast principals. We know it's true in our case. I have been a part of this school several years longer than you. *I'm* planning to stick around."

"You shouldn't listen to everything that old bat says. Now get back to your classroom. It's almost time for fourth hour." Bart's level gaze dared me to call him on his characterization of Lenore. The steady look told me his comment was a bargaining chip for me. What I'd said would stay in the office if what he'd said did as well.

My step was lighter leaving than it had been going in. I slowed as I went down the hall to the reception area. I didn't want to turn around, but small thoughts kept me back in Bart's office. I was getting braver the longer I taught. When I'd started teaching, I would certainly have broken down and cried if the principal had talked to me as Bart had.

But maybe I had been too brave, foolhardy, even. When the colonel had been killed, I felt as though all of us at that rehearsal had been in danger. Now, I wondered if I was.

I had dealt with students before who came in to my classroom convinced that I had nothing to teach them and that I served at their pleasure. Although they'd never said, "My parents own you," they conveyed that attitude. I was afraid my demeanor had projected the same message in Bart's office. While what I had reported hearing from Lenore was true, it wasn't politic to share it with Bart.

And he seemed to have taken my comment especially hard. Had he blanched a bit, looked rather green at the gills, when I mentioned that my tenure at Quanah was longer than his? Was Bart scared? Was he scared enough to lash out?

Two competing theories played in my head. Perhaps the Beamers, unhappy with Bart's solution to their problem with the colonel, had solved the problem themselves. Or maybe Bart, unable to deal effectively with whatever the problem was, had eliminated the colonel, and thus the problem? Suspects were multiplying like ungraded papers on my desk.

The perfect person to answer my questions stood at the front counter at the end of the hall. Mac leaned toward Carolyn, who stood behind the counter, fluttering like a butterfly at Mac's attention.

"Sheriff, aren't you back soon!" When I heard myself greet him, I cringed.

"Reg, I just had to clarify a few things. I left Shrimp to look after Chris down at the jail."

"How's he doing?"

"Shrimp is a fine officer. I trust him implicitly." At my pursed lip reaction, he grinned and said, "Chris is doing fine."

"I didn't think you'd take murder so lightly."

"Reg, I never take murder lightly." His grin had disappeared. "Can you tell me anything about the props you were using for the show? Where'd you get them, that sort of thing?"

Carolyn looked a little disappointed that Mac's attention had shifted to me, but she went back to her business with the binder, only half listening to our conversation.

"It depends. Some of the stuff we pulled from our inventory backstage. We always borrow a few bits and pieces, of course. I hate to buy if someone can lend us a piece."

"The particular item I'm interested in is that knife. Well, it's more a pretty thing than a real knife, isn't it, with jewels and such on it?"

"The little dagger Libby lent us?"

Mac simply nodded for me to go on.

"Libby lent us a dagger. I told you about it last night."

"And...?"

"It was a gift. To Libby, I mean. Something a friend of hers had found in Italy." I was usually more articulate, but Mac, even in his professional capacity, was sending out very masculine vibes and I was picking them up. He had an unfair advantage in this exchange. "Didn't I tell you about this already?"

"I'm just following up. You told me that your stage manager locked it up backstage."

I nodded. "The last time I saw the knife, Rick took it away and locked it up in one of the cabinets backstage. He's very conscientious and careful about locking things away that have any potential for danger. I'd hardly call it a knife, anyway. It's more like a letter opener."

"It may be a murder weapon." Mac pulled me away from Carolyn at the counter and the reporters still waiting. All of them had perked up and sat on the edges of their seats.

I felt the blood drain from my face and a swift, hot flush spread down my chest. "A murder weapon?"

"If it didn't finish the job, it started it," he said. My expression must have indicated how sickening I found that idea, because Mac's face softened. "I don't want you to focus on the scene right now, but tell me who had access to that piece during your rehearsal."

"Well, you saw the whole cast of characters when you arrived. Every student there was backstage at some point."

Mac rubbed a finger across his chin. "Yeah, that's what I figured. I think that Rick may not be as dependable as you think. I have someone saying they saw Chris playing with that knife backstage."

"Who?"

Shaking his head, Mac said, "That's not important. I just needed to confirm it was possible Chris might have had access to the dagger."

"Letter opener," I corrected him.

"Murder weapon."

The reality of the situation made me stop. Rick was a responsible stage manager who usually did exactly as I asked him to, but he was also a teenager. Other students might have gotten their hands on the letter opener before he put it away.

I sighed. "Look, two things occur to me."

Mac nodded for me to go on.

"If the kids messed around with the letter open—the thing— they might have taken pictures with it, and you could check their social media to see."

"We'll be doing that. What else?"

"I forgot about someone else who was at rehearsal."

"Damn it, when were you gonna tell me?" Mac's volume made Carolyn look up and glare at him. The reporters edged even closer to the edge of their seats, almost falling off.

"As soon as I saw you, which is now. Stephen Keener was there, just for a minute, talking to the colonel."

"Anything unusual about their conversation?"

"It got loud," I said. "Loud enough that it drew my focus."

"What was the problem?"

"I don't know. They were at the back of the auditorium, so I couldn't hear exactly what they were saying. They raised their voices; I turned around. When they saw they'd disturbed our rehearsal, Stephen left and the colonel apologized and went back to grading his papers."

"Thank you." Mac took out his notebook and made a note.

"We're going back to rehearsal today after school. Four o'clock. Can we talk after school if there's anything else? There's an English class waiting on me even as we speak."

"Then I'll let you go, but only because I know we'll speak again soon. What's that line from your play that's so appropriate?"

"Parting is such sweet sorrow?"

"No, I was thinking, 'A rose by any other name would smell as sweet.' That's some perfume you're working today."

My ears buzzed, and I heard Carolyn snort. Mac walked out the glass door of the office. I was certain the little scene between Mac and me would soon be replayed for a wider audience. The reporters didn't care about a little flirtation, but being witnessed by Carolyn was worse than being caught on camera.

She could embellish.

CHAPTER TEN

After watching the last students bolt from my room for home at the end of last hour, I stopped at Lenore's classroom on my way to rehearsal. I found her bending over papers at her desk. She offered me tea as soon as I walked in her room. I waved off the offer.

"No, even Sleepytime couldn't calm my nerves right now. I have, along with the mediocre papers from my drama class, several that are outstanding but not original," I told her. "I've got to deal with an outbreak of cheating."

Lenore raised one arched, expressive eyebrow at me. Her dark brows contrasted with her prematurely gray hair, worn in a bob. She kept her patrician profile turned to me and continued to check the tests in front of her, running a pen held in one graceful, well-manicured hand down the right-hand side of each paper and then flipping it over to go the next. Skim, flip. Skim, flip. The silky kimono-like sleeves of her blouse didn't hinder her rhythm, only emphasized her smooth, steady movement.

"They've used the Internet for more than just research," she said, laying her pen on the desk and leaning back in her chair. She propped her fingers together in a steeple and touched them to her lips. "And you plan to make an example of them."

"I have to do something." Dropping my bag on the floor, I curled up on a beanbag chair near her desk. I'd felt girly enough that morning to wear a skirt, but I'd paired the A-line gray flannel with a pair of black tights in a nod to the chilly February weather. Trying to sit on the beanbag without flashing the empty room like a Hollywood starlet offered a challenge. "I have done something. I called a slate of parents about it, and Bart heard about it."

"He didn't like your response?"

"No."

"Well, I don't know the circumstances yet. But I suspect you're being self-righteous for a perfectly good reason." Lenore's eyes laughed even when the rest of her face didn't.

"And on top of that, you know I had to replace Chris. He's not playing Romeo anymore."

"Sheriff Snyder's actions have taken that beyond your control anyway. I suppose the colonel didn't find theater a suitably masculine pastime?" Lenore had set aside the graded papers and gave me her full attention.

"He made that very clear to me the day he showed up at rehearsal. The day he got himself killed."

"That's blaming the victim."

"There seems to be plenty of blame to go around, and none of it makes me feel any safer. The sheriff thinks Chris did it, but I know Chris wasn't out of my sight long enough to stab his father."

"Who was?"

"Abby was messing around backstage for part of rehearsal yesterday."

"What motive might she have?"

I shrugged. "The colonel gave her a bad grade in geometry."

"And a bad grade was enough to set her off? Yes, I can see why, if you believe that, you wouldn't feel safe. You've called her a cheater and let her parents know the truth."

"You know what they say around here. 'It's no good to lock the barn after the horse was stolen.'" I twisted a little, still trying to get comfortable in the inhospitable chair. "I don't want to believe Abby did it. At first, she couldn't look me in the eye when I called her out for copying. How could she face the colonel and stay strong enough to stab him? But she got defiant."

"Defiant how?"

I thought about it. "It wasn't what she said so much as how she said it. Her parents are upset with her when she gets bad grades. She's trying to play basketball and do the play. She's under a lot of pressure."

"Pressure a lot of our best kids feel." Lenore leaned forward. "If not Abby, then who?"

"Her parents?" I stood up from the beanbag and hesitated just a second, my feet planted wide apart, to get my balance.

"Could they?"

"Like I told the sheriff, the kids prop doors open all the time during rehearsal. The Beamers would have had no problem getting in to the auditorium."

"Motive?"

"Grades again. I thought Jessica—that's Abby's Mom—I thought Jessica and I had a pleasant conversation about Abby's issue and then she hung up on me and dialed Bart to tattle."

"Tattletales don't usually carry knives," Lenore said.

"Whoever killed the colonel didn't have to. They used the letter opener we had backstage." I sighed and sat down in a chair more forgiving than the beanbag I'd escaped. "The Beamers might want the best for their daughter and be willing to take their complaints to the next level, but I don't think they'd kill over a math grade."

"What kind of detective are you? You keep giving people the benefit of the doubt. That's no way to find the culprit!"

"Well, I'm a silver-lining person."

Both of us were quiet for a moment.

I broke the silence.

"Bart."

"Lincoln? Our principal? Why on earth would he want to kill the colonel?"

"He had to field a lot of calls about the colonel's teaching. The Beamers weren't happy with me, but they weren't happy with the colonel either. Every time they made a phone call to Bart, he had to watch time he could have spent planning his next fishing trip slip away."

Lenore snorted. "Bart Lincoln is about the most ineffectual human being I've ever worked with. You know the Peter Principle, right? People rise to the level of their incompetence? He's right there."

"But being a bad principal might mean that murder looked like a reasonable plan."

"What else you got?"

I looked up, scanning the tiles in the drop ceiling. Some of them had been decorated by seniors from previous years. One of the grads had decorated a rectangle with an image of two wrestlers grappling. The art reminded me of what I'd almost forgotten to tell Mac.

"Keener!" I cried.

"What do you mean?"

"Stephen Keener was in the auditorium the day of the murder and had some kind of argument with the colonel."

"What were they arguing about?"

"I couldn't hear. I don't think they were arguing about math pedagogy, that's for sure."

"Maybe one of Keener's wrestlers was having problems in the colonel's class," Lenore said.

"Is that worth murdering someone?"

"Well, it wouldn't be for me." Lenore had leaned back in her chair and was sipping tea while she pondered the list of suspects I'd offered. "Who knows what the conflict really involved? Put a person in the middle of pressures coming from all sides, well, it can change them. Let's say Stephen's best wrestler—"

"Danny?" I said. Danny was a senior boy who walked around like a coiled spring. At a little over five feet, he was lean and well-muscled, the result of a Spartan diet and intense workouts.

"Yes, let's say Danny isn't performing well in math and won't be eligible to wrestle."

"I'd think that Stephen should be yelling at Danny, not the colonel. But if Danny's parents want him to do well because he needs the scholarship, and he had to wrestle so the college scouts can see him, or, and this speaks more to Stephen's motivation, what if Stephen has some college he's trying to impress because he wants to coach there? And what if he can't get his best wrestler on the mat?"

"None of this is useful. You should just let the sheriff handle it and get on with your play. They're going to let you back in the auditorium today?"

"No, we're going to push back the tables and chairs in my room and work there."

"And you've got a new Romeo. So who is second choice? Lab would make a great Romeo," Lenore said.

"No, he was born to play Mercutio. And besides, he already believes he's the star of the show. I had to go to my second choice. Adam King."

Lenore nodded. "Adam's a good, dependable boy. He'll do the job, but he is more of a brute than Chris. Not just physically, I think. I overheard some of the colonel's comments in the lounge as to his doubts about theater being an appropriate outlet for Chris. I believe baseball season looms, and as soon as Chris turned in his tights, he was going to pick up a cup."

I hid a grin behind my hand. "Crude."

"But accurate. Chris wanted to please you, but he also wanted to please his father. I suspect he spent much of his time on such a tightrope." We were both silent, considering the stress that navigating life on such a narrow path would mean for a teenager.

I didn't have a context for Lenore's comment. My parents were always proud of me. When I was a teenager, it hadn't seemed hard to get their approval. The conflict between Chris and his father reminded me of another conflict the colonel had.

"What about Libby?" I said.

"Our Libby?"

"She had an ongoing conflict with the colonel."

"If Bart had moved them apart, the conflict would have disappeared."

"But he didn't, and they kept at each other."

"Libby is the most peaceful person I know. The idea of that little woman driving a knife—"

"A letter opener."

Lenore shuddered. "I stand corrected. A letter opener? I can't see her using anything against a human being. She'd roll up in a ball at the first sign of conflict."

"I enjoy it more when we agree with each other. It makes me feel as though my high opinion of myself is justified."

Lenore laughed, but sobered as she said, "You're wrong about the murderer, but right about the plagiarist."

"Abby?"

"Yes. Just be gentle with her parents. They are very quick to make trips up here, and they've already called Bart about how you've handled the whole thing."

"Thanks for the warning." I shouldered my bag. "I have to go to rehearsal."

"Keep to your lane. You've got a play to direct."

CHAPTER ELEVEN

Walking into the auditorium at the end of the school day was always like walking through an invisible door that led to a secret cave where strange rituals were enacted.

One day, I found a row of girls laid out on the stage, heads tilted backward over the lip, urging me to join them and get a new perspective on the world. When I stretched out beside them and tilted my head back, I felt lightheaded and started grinning. The aisles tilted down toward the pebbled ceiling, making me dizzy.

Other days, a ragged circle of students on the stage and sitting in the first row of seats would be engaged in a game called Mafia.

Mafia was a complex game that began with a deck of cards and a narrator with a vivid, if gruesome, imagination. Each player would draw a card. Whoever drew a certain card became the mafia. The mafioso's goal was to murder another player without getting caught. Another card made the bearer the night watchman, who looked around for evidence of the perpetrator. All the other players were townspeople, and, like the night watchman, potential victims.

But murder wasn't a game anymore, and when I arrived at rehearsal, the cast and crew were quiet. Meeting for rehearsal in my room had added to their disorientation, and they pressed close to each other like the baby chicks in the incubator on my grandmother's kitchen floor. The chicks had always chirped as they tumbled over each other, but my students sat quiet and still.

"Okay, guys, let's get stuff moved back so we've got room to work."

The students moved to push tables and chairs back and clear a space in the center of my room. I dug my director's binder out of my bag and sat on the edge of a table facing the empty area they'd created.

"Ms. Murphy. I don't think it's normal to put on a play at the scene of a crime," Abby said.

Her tone was short. I couldn't tell if the tension was from being so close to where Slayton had died or if her clipped delivery betrayed her pique at me over the plagiarism incident.

"And I don't appreciate you ratting me out to my parents." A few nods of agreement told me she'd been complaining to the others.

"Abby, this isn't the time or the place. I talked to you privately about the paper." I hoped she would take the hint and drop the matter. I didn't want an audience for another discussion, and I knew she didn't either.

Abby's parents had made the trip to see Bart, and their pilgrimage to the principal's office had embarrassed her, although she'd been responsible for the whole situation in the first place. Parents were bound to be shocked to find out their kids weren't perfect. They usually failed to appreciate how crafty they can be.

My instinct told me Abby had done some preemptive spinning to her parents before I spoke to her mother. Abby didn't have any reason to trust me. If she told her parents first, she could control how they saw the incident, and she knew her description of herself as the victim of an irrational English teacher would be better received than plagiarist. I don't think she believed me when I tried to tell her she'd made a bad choice but wasn't a bad person.

I had a student caught in a similar situation a couple of years before. As a freshman, he'd plagiarized a ridiculously simple assignment, and I'd called him on it. Four years later, he won state championships in debate and extemporaneous speaking. His achievement took a lot of work and dedication that could not be faked. My experience told me kids could make bad choices and recover from them. Abby had not recovered yet, and why would she have? She hadn't had time to deal with our conflict while the drama of the colonel's death was playing out.

"If you'd like to leave, go ahead. We're just blocking Romeo and Friar Laurence's scene today. The nurse isn't on the call sheet."

Abby nodded and gathered her backpack and jacket. She pressed her lips together as she disappeared out the door. The rest of the kids looked at each other without saying anything, and then looked to me for direction.

"We'll get back to the show with a little scene. Act II, scene 3. Romeo goes to Friar Laurence to arrange the marriage."

"He's moving pretty fast, isn't he?" Nicole asked.

An unidentified voice spoke up. "Not as fast as Lincoln Collier." I couldn't see who had spoken.

"Lincoln and I are just friends," Nicole said. She flipped through her script to find the scene.

"Now, anyway." said the voice.

Nicole's head whipped around at that rejoinder. I tried to wrest the rehearsal back on track.

"So that means we really only need Adam and Cody. The rest of you can cut out." Normally, most of them wouldn't be at today's rehearsal. I had coded the schedule to show the students when they were needed so only the required actors, the stage manager, and the crew would show up. Today almost everyone had. Many of them didn't want to go home to empty houses to wait for parents to get home from work. The auditorium could be a cold, empty hangar at times, but today's space seemed to be offering comfort by forcing them closer. "Of course, if you stay, you'll need to do warm-ups with us."

My casual warning didn't prompt any exits.

"Rick, put 'em through their paces." I needed to focus on Romeo and Friar Laurence, but I couldn't move away from the thought of Chris sitting behind bars. I knew Carolyn had meant to be reassuring when she mentioned the interior design efforts of the former sheriff's wife, but the curtains and potted plants could not have made Chris any more comfortable in jail.

"We're playing this scene center, guys. Friar, you need some sort of business as Romeo enters. I've got a rough table to put up there, a couple of chairs. You need to putter."

"Oh, I can putter." My Friar Laurence smirked. Cody looked like a farm boy, big and milk-fed, his bulky form straining the overalls he wore over a t-shirt with a questionable motto.

Cody spent a lot of his time mucking out the chicken houses for his family's business, but he also put in time at the computer, downloading music and playing Fortnite. Cody moved among several worlds: the farm where he lived, the hills of the imaginary world he played in, the subculture of hip-hop aficionados—small but intense in Quanah—and the little world of Shakespeare's we were creating on our stage. He would look at home in the rough brown robe I'd designed and his mother was running up on her machine, but I'd have a hard time separating him from the gimme cap he perpetually wore.

Rick had posted himself, script in hand, downstage right, and volunteered, "Maybe he could be potting plants or something. He'd have something to do with his hands."

"That's great. Cody, pantomime the potting for now. We'll have some pots and dirt for you next time we run this scene. Let's get Romeo in here."

Rick, sitting on the floor between me and the performance area, made a note.

"Where do I enter, Ms. Murphy?" Adam clutched

his script, kneading the pages like a ball of pizza dough as he stood center stage. Cody focused on potting a forest of plants in imaginary pots and ignored Adam.

"The concert curtain will be closed, and the doorway will be center, so just slip through the curtains and enter there." Adam nodded.

A rustle behind me turned my head, and I saw Libby entering the room with an armload of books.

"Are you okay, Reg? I knew you'd be back at work and I thought I'd bring the books I promised."

"It's fine. I think we're approaching normal."

"Normal is relative, I suppose." Libby dumped the books on the table beside me and took a spot on the slanting floor of the aisle for herself. "Just some old books I turned up in my library for you. Costume stuff, mostly. I brought some things for the kids to try on. When should I do that?"

Flipping to the calendar in my notebook, I told her, "The day after tomorrow almost the entire cast is called. Can you be here then? I'd love to get the girls into those long skirts. I don't think they have a clue what it will mean to drag that kind of weight around with them." Adam and Cody had stalled, so I told them, "Walk through the scene from the top. Just see what seems natural. I know you're there."

"Adam's filling in well, isn't he?" Libby continued our conversation under her breath.

"Well, he's not Chris, but I'm lucky I had a guy at all. I didn't have that many choices when I'd cast all the roles."

"Have you talked to Chris?"

"Today?"

"Since Shrimp and Mac staged their takedown."

"Mac's not so bad ... and Shrimp's just a little overzealous." I hoped my defense of Shrimp would keep Libby from thinking I might be partial to Mac.

"What's clouding your eyes? There's a civil way to handle this stuff, and banging a kid into the lockers in the hall is not the way to do it. I imagine Chris has had to deal with enough of that to hold his peace, but that doesn't mean he deserves it."

"Chris hasn't really been a brawler."

"But his dad was. By profession."

My jaw dropped. "Do you mean the colonel beat Chris?"

Libby shrugged. "Retired military. A total control freak. Chris wasn't the regulation teenage son."

"Don't you think it's a little dangerous to imply anything when Chris is under suspicion for his dad's murder? Someone could hear and think he had a motive beyond his dad forcing him to quit the play."

"I've told only you, and you're not going to repeat what I just said to anyone." Libby stared into my eyes. "Are you? You're sweet on Mac, aren't you?"

I flushed a bit, but didn't answer.

"I guess I better keep my mouth shut."

"I won't repeat anything to Mac. He's handling the investigation on his own. I don't want to help him hang Chris. I know he didn't do it."

"You know?" Libby's eyes widened at my firmness.

"Well, okay, it's not like I saw the real murderer, I'm just convinced Chris isn't it."

Libby stood up, smoothing the wrinkles from her skirt and slipping her feet back into the clunky slides she had kicked off as she sat down. "Me, too.

I'm thinking about trying to see Chris. Do you think Shrimp will let us in?"

"I think tonight will be a good time to go visiting. If Shrimp is on days, then someone else will tend the desk tonight. It's worth a try."

"Meet me there about seven and we'll try our luck."

"Okay. I better get back to those boys. They think I've abandoned them."

"Well, they seem to be able to entertain themselves."

Libby left and I turned back to the students. Adam and Cody had taken advantage of my distraction to gather an audience for a different kind of performance. Cody was "freestyling" a rap version of the Montague and Capulet saga. Adam spluttered, backing him up beatbox style.

Damp beatbox style.

Cody's words flowed as if he'd written and polished his impromptu twenty-first century take on the ancient grudge.

"Two families met here on this street,
Threatening to leave dead meat.
If the parents find what's going down,
Someone's leaving, out of town.
Juliet and Romeo,
keep it on the d-low,
the heat that flamed them up one night
makes 'em twisted lovers out of sight."

Adam jerkily stabbed the air in a bad imitation of a gangsta. They'd drawn the rest of the kids toward them, and everyone was focused on Cody's jiggling form.

"Cheese it, it's the coppers," I yelled, and a couple of dozen pairs of squinted eyes and curled-lipped faces turned to me.

"Ms. Murphy," Cody slowly enunciated, "you are not even in the right century with that slang. 'Coppers'? You're old, but not that old." He crossed his arms over his rounded tummy and leaned back, unable to keep his smirk in place, grinning at my inept effort to be cool.

I had made Cody laugh. Maybe not for the right reasons, but it felt good.

"What have you done with the scene while my back was turned?"

"Oh, we'll show you. We didn't want to overdo it. We're trying to keep it fresh, ya know."

"Scatter," I said to the cast and crew. "Show me what you've got, guys."

Adam and Cody managed to keep me focused as they ran through the scene, and by the time I'd given them a couple of suggestions, heard Cody's impromptu Julia Child impression as he potted imaginary herbs, reminded Adam to stay turned out to the audience because the back of his head just wasn't as expressive as his face, and made Cody run a lap around halls because he was chewing gum during rehearsal, it was time to go. Rick, the first one there every day and the last student out, had gone.

I tried to keep Libby's books closed neatly so I wouldn't damage them as I wrestled them into my bag along with the night's grading, but one of them opened and a photo fell out. About five by seven inches, the picture was a black and white print like a newspaper might use. I looked at it but didn't recognize whatever event it documented. Along the left, a row of National Guardsmen stood with rifles held diagonally in front of them, their chins up, eyes unfocused but forward. Along the right, a group of young people stood with protest signs in hand.

At first, I thought the scene had to be an anti-war protest of some kind, but the civilian's clothes were wrong and the slogans on the signs were decrying environmental issues instead of the war. Maybe Libby had been using it as a bookmark. She was a history teacher, so she probably had all kinds of ephemera related to her class. I slipped the photo back into the book.

I couldn't help flipping through the volumes again before trying to fit them into my bag like Tetris pieces. A couple of the books were foreign editions, and my mouth watered at the soft leather covers. The endpapers swirled with peacock-like blues and green. The bookplates in each book bore *EH* in elaborate script. But the name underneath didn't match Libby's.

"Elinor Huntington"

Maybe a relative had given her the books? But Huntington wasn't her family name. I knew she'd never been married. I guessed it could be an aunt on her mother's side. Or she might have just bought the book at a thrift store or estate sale. Libby's genealogy wasn't the point, the contents of the book were. The name still nagged at me as I left. I couldn't quite place it, and my consciousness poked at the six hard syllables as though they were a worrisome tooth.

CHAPTER TWELVE

Carolyn had told me about the last sheriff's wife's efforts to cheer up the office, but I wasn't prepared for the crowded little room I stepped into. By the time I made it to the police station, it was approaching dark outside, but the public room I stepped into when I entered the jail glowed brighter than a kindergarten classroom. Despite the institutional gray paint on the cinder block walls, I saw a lot of evidence that someone—the last sheriff's wife, I assumed—had been addicted to yarn and, instead of seeking help in a twelve-step program, had tortured myriad skeins of low-end acrylic into decorations for the little office.

Crocheted clowns bracketed the professional manuals housed on shelves along one wall. Yellow-checked gingham material had been smocked and cross-stitched into puffy valances over the windows. The orange vinyl couch and chair in the waiting area were filled with pillows covered with elaborate crochet. The magazines littering the coffee table were scattered over an intricately worked doily of some kind, and even the desk had a pencil holder covered in a Fair Isle pattern and a paperweight made of a rock with a knitted cover. I didn't just find the amount of needlework crowding the place disturbing; the palette bothered me, too. The colors screamed past cheerful into hysterical. To see the grinning dolls knit of Day-Glo pinks and yellows was to understand why some people were terrified of clowns.

Shrimp sat at the desk between me and the door leading back to the holding cells.

Damn.

In a department as small as Quanah's, Shrimp and Mac worked some long shifts. Why couldn't Mac be sitting there? Of course, if he had been, I might have lost interest in visiting Chris.

Libby wasn't standing outside when I pulled up to the jail, so I assumed she'd decided to meet me in the waiting room. No sign of her. I'd to deal with Shrimp on my own. If I stalled and waited for Libby to show, Shrimp might get difficult and not let me in to see Chris.

"Deputy Standfield," I said, not committing to a real greeting. I had to balance my intense dislike for him with the need to remain polite so he would let me see Chris.

"Ms. Murphy."

I waited a beat or two to respond while I decided whether flat-out asking to see Chris would work or whether I needed to butter up the deputy. I couldn't think about the implications of that phrase without shuddering.

"I hope you are not here to report a crime you've been a victim of." He was formal, but grammatically incorrect. The English teacher part of my brain rewrote his sentence to get rid of the preposition at the end, but I didn't comment aloud.

"No, I'm safe and sound," I said. "Thank you for your concern."

"Then how may I help you this evening?"

"I brought some things for Chris. I wasn't happy with the selection at the Pik 'n' Git, but I thought he might appreciate something to read."

"Trying to get his mind off things, are you?" Shrimp sniffed.

"I don't think a couple of computer magazines will take his mind off his father's murder." A little too saucy. Shrimp took offense.

"Those computer books might pose a threat. These kids can get up to a lot with those machines."

"Shrimp, you've got him locked in a cell with no computer and no phone! Even if he made his way out here, that machine you've got would not catch his eye. Will you let me see Chris, please?" My patience had run out quickly when confronted with his stupidity. Tacking on that *please* was as difficult as swallowing a dose of castor oil, but the phrase might lubricate the social interaction.

"A teacher ought to keep better control over her emotions. There's no need to get testy." Shrimp stood up. I shifted from one foot to the other and watched him take a set of keys from his pocket like Scrooge McDuck might take out a gold piece. "You can't stay in here all night, you know. Fifteen minutes is the limit. Let me look at those magazines."

I handed them over, my compliance an admission he had let me win this round, and watched him riffle through the pages. His eyes frequently shifted from the articles back to me, watching for any sign I might be up to something. I cultivated a blank look. Smiling would only make him more suspicious, and looking aggrieved would make him more officious. Shrimp had the keys to the door between Chris and me. So I waited.

"I guess you can take these magazines on in with you. Everything checks out. I'll lead you back there, but remember: I've got an eye on my watch."

"Yes, sir."

He rattled the keys as he opened the door. Was that some kind of display? Was the size of a man's key ring a kind of marker for his potency?

Enough of my irritation. I took a few deep breaths to shake off the tension interacting with Shrimp had created. Chris deserved a sunnier demeanor when I faced him.

Beyond the locked entry was a short hallway. On one side, a door opened into an office with a display of certificates on one wall and a framed print of a Remington painting on another. Mac's office, I guessed. Across from his space was a small conference room with a table and eight chairs. The yarn addict hadn't made any inroads back here. At the end of the little hall, another hall made a *T* of it. Along the top of the *T* were three barred cells, each with a simple set of bunks, a sink, and a metal toilet. Chris sat in the center cell.

He was alone. Parked on the bottom bunk, dressed in the clothes he'd left school in earlier, but with no belt and no laces in his shoes. His hands were clasped, elbows on his knees, head down so his hair swung forward and hid his profile. I walked down the hall, grateful that Shrimp kept silent as he backed out. Even he must realize what an impact I felt to see the boy who had been sitting in my class a week ago sitting behind bars. The door clicked closed and the same click came from my throat as I tried to say Chris's name. I swallowed hard and tried again.

"Chris?"

"Ms. Murphy?" He turned his head only enough to register my presence, and I stood at the bars of the cell.

"I brought you something to read."

"Thanks." He reached for the magazines and tossed them beside him on the mattress without looking at them.

"I wanted to see how you were doing."

"I'm okay." His voice lacked expression. His words were brief. Happy energy usually kept Chris bouncing, but now he sat on the bunk like a puppet whose strings had been cut.

"Is there anything I can do?"

"Will you talk to them and tell them I didn't kill my father? Why do they think I would? Ms. Murphy, I could never kill anyone!" I reached through the bars to take his hand and we stood face to face.

"I don't think they'll listen to me, Chris." I knew Shrimp wouldn't. Mac might listen if I pleaded Chris's case, but he'd make his own judgment, no matter the attraction between us. "The best we can do is wait for the truth to come out."

"I hope you're comfortable waiting out there." He returned to the bunk.

Chris had hit me where it hurt. He was in a cell and I was walking around free. I couldn't just be upset they'd taken him in; I had to do something to get him out. "Was anyone upset with your dad?"

Chris didn't respond.

"Your dad had an argument with Coach Keener at rehearsal that day. What would they have been fighting about?"

Chris shrugged.

"I can help you, but you've got to help yourself. Think about it."

"I don't have any idea. My dad was always upset with somebody up there at the school. Keener, Ms. Hoffman, Lincoln. Every night at supper we'd have to hear about something that had gone down that day."

"Why would he be upset with other teachers?"

"Different things. He thought Coach Keener was trying to cheat the system to make sure his best guys got to wrestle, you know."

I nodded.

"And Miss Hoffman was too easy on us, he said. Her classes were always noisy, and Dad kept telling her it was disrupting his. I loved Ms. Hoffman's class, we did cool stuff in there all the time, but when I told my Dad that, he shut me down with some spiel about citizenship and following the rules so I didn't end up on the wrong end of a gun at some protest." Chris shook his head. "It didn't make much sense, so I just quit trying to tell him how I felt."

I waited a moment before I asked about someone else. "Did he ever mention the Beamers?"

"Abby's folks?" Chris looked up, trying to remember, but his shoulders still had a defeated slouch. He shook his head. "No, I don't remember him talking about them. It was usually someone that worked at the school."

"Gotcha." The list I'd been making had just been reduced. So the colonel had problems with other staff members? Mac should be asking these questions. If he didn't, I'd have to.

I heard a whimper and focused again on Chris, still sitting on the cell's bunk. "Ms. Murphy, I'm sorry. I've just never done this before. I don't know how to do this. If you see my Mom, tell her I love her no matter what."

"Your mom knows you love her."

Chris nodded.

Shrimp opened the door.

"Time's up, Ms. Murphy."

I nodded to the deputy as I left, but couldn't think of a thing to say. Opening the door to the street, I almost ran into Ginny Slayton.

"Ms. Murphy! Have you been in to see Chris?" Pale in the lowering dusk of the evening, Ginny clutched a cloth coat close around her, shivering but gracious. "He admires you so much."

"I just dropped off some magazines. Chris didn't seem to want to talk."

"He'll need to do some talking to me." Out of the shadows behind Ginny a reedy voice emerged. The body attached to the voice was that of a slight, skinny, younger man in an ill-fitting corduroy jacket over a button-down shirt and a pair of Dockers. His hair had been cut so recently he looked sheared, and the hiking boots he wore with the ensemble were the final touch in an outfit that communicated "I rarely dress up and when I do, it turns out all wrong." His tie was an outdated, squared off natural fiber rectangle that he had ineptly knotted, and it hung below his open collar, which revealed a yellowish undershirt. I hoped the jaundiced T-shirt was a function of the dim light and not his laundry habits.

"Oh, Ms. Murphy, let me make the introductions! Ms. Murphy, this is Richard Murray. When my parents heard about Chris's trouble, they called their law firm, and they were kind enough to send Ricky down here to help us out. Ricky, Regina is the drama teacher over at the high school."

Ricky was not the biggest gun in the arsenal. His wardrobe shouted his status. I suspected that Ginny's family had old money if they could call out the dogs so easily. I had to wonder if Mr. Murray had appeared because the firm thought little of Ginny's family but had to send a token to keep up appearances or if her parents were only going through the motions and had asked the firm "to send just anyone."

"Where is home, Mr. Murray?" I asked.

"I'm from the Dallas office. Ginny's folks live out in Asheville, North Carolina—"

"I was born and raised in the Carolinas, I think I told you, and Momma and Daddy still live out there." Ginny offered.

Ricky ignored her, "—a bit too far to come on such short notice. I work for Lomax, West, and Alcorn.

"First year?" I was curious, and knew if I crossed the line he would clam up. It never hurt to ask, and being rebuffed wasn't that painful either. Besides, I'd always believed knowledge was power.

"Yes. I'm an Okie originally. Got my juris doctorate from the University of Tulsa. Passed the bar here, too. Still working on my Texas bona fides."

"I hope you can help Chris. I can tell the last few days have been tough for him, losing his father and then being accused of the crime."

"Chris needs to know that the law helps those who help themselves." Murray's response seemed an odd statement from a defense lawyer.

"Have you met Chris, Mr. Murray?" I knew he hadn't, but I wanted him to realize he didn't know anything about the teenage boy waiting for rescue in the jail behind me. "Because Chris is a wonderful kid. I hope you aren't presuming he's guilty of what they've accused him of here. In fact, he told me his dad had several conflicts with other people on the staff at the school."

Murray only nodded in response.

"Of course Ricky doesn't think Chris killed the colonel!" Ginny fluttered to clear away the conflict rising between the lawyer and me. "I'd insist he turn around and go back to Dallas right this minute if he thought any such thing. My son needs some kind of protection right now, and I couldn't turn anywhere but to my parents. They have been very thoughtful to ask their friends to send someone to help."

I hadn't thought about Ginny's financial situation, but it couldn't be good. Even with his military pension and teacher's salary, Slayton couldn't have been making much. I guessed any assets the couple had were difficult if not impossible to get out while his murder was being investigated. The Slayton's finances weren't any of my business, but I was worried about Chris.

"I'm sure Mr. Murray will do a fine job, Ginny. If you'll excuse me, I have to get home. I've got a stack of papers to grade before I sleep."

"Pleasure to meet you, Ms. Murphy," the lawyer said.

"Thank you. Let me know, Ginny, if there's anything at all I can do for you and Chris."

"Thank you, Ms. Murphy."

I watched the two of them disappear into the jail and crossed my fingers for Chris. His mother seemed to be the kind of woman who had always had someone else to solve the petty troubles that cropped up in life like weeds in a garden. I hoped Ricky Murray could solve this problem for her.

CHAPTER THIRTEEN

A townhouse in Tulsa would have suited Lenore's elegant, sleek style, but her husband Will Roland was a contractor, and he used their home as a showroom. Lenore's complaints about some new addition or gadget Will had added to the house sometimes amused me and sometimes grated, but she delivered the complaints in a fawning tone that betrayed how much she cared about him.

When I arrived Tuesday evening, Lenore wasn't complaining. She was missing Will. Every lamp and overhead light in the house shone. I followed Lenore into the kitchen that ran along the back of the single-floor ranch house.

"I know it looks like an open house, but I can't stand dark corners when Will's not here."

An island with a concrete top separated the generous galley at one end of the kitchen from a living area on the other. The orange-red upholstery of the overstuffed conversation group seemed to glitter in the firelight. The colors of the living area picked up the warm browns of the cabinets and the shiny copper of the pans hanging in the kitchen. Lenore set out a basket of tiny buttery Italian toasts and a small crock of her homemade tapenade on the S curve of the island.

"Just throw your coat on the couch, there. What would you like to drink? The tapenade's a little salty." Lenore said.

"I can't. I'm too upset about Chris being thrown in that drunk tank. I'm gritting my teeth so hard the wine would never make it down my throat."

"I have a nice Chardonnay Will brought back from California on his last trip." Lenore wagged the bottle at me. "A little wine is just what you need. And how are you going to tell me everything with your teeth clenched?"

"You've got me. That sounds wonderful. Is that where he's working now, in California?" I joined her at the counter and sat down on one of the tall mahogany stools. I slathered some of the tapenade on a disk of bread and bit into the salty olive medley.

"No, he's gone to visit a cabinetmaker in Vermont or New Hampshire. The one that looks like an apostrophe, not a comma. I can't keep them straight." Lenore poured the wine into two delicate goblets and handed me one. "He's got an idea the guy can do the cabinets for that new house out on the lake."

I accepted the glass and watched Lenore putter around the kitchen. Making small talk, I asked, "Do you know how Cody has an odd store of factoids he likes to share?"

"Cody Mathers or Cody Wallace?"

"Mathers. I don't know Cody Wallace."

"He's a senior. You can't miss him. He's as big as those bulls he raises for FFA." Lenore blinked and added, "Terrible thing to say. I mean it in the nicest way. He's a bull of a boy. But nice."

"Well, Mathers was spouting off at rehearsal, and he said Oklahoma has more shoreline than Florida. Do you believe that?"

"All these lakes." She opened the oven and poked at the chicken roasting there. "Cody is a font of information. Was he at rehearsal the day you found the colonel?"

"No, he's playing the Friar and wasn't called that day. I couldn't imagine Cody having anything to do with the colonel's death though."

"*I* can't imagine Chris had anything to do with it either, but he's sitting in jail right now." Lenore picked at the tapenade and sipped some wine without sitting down.

"Ginny's family sent a lawyer. I met him when I went to see Chris."

"Oh, dear. How was the boy?"

I shrugged.

"All alone in that dreadful cell."

"The cell is rather festive." I described the crafty accoutrements meant to brighten the cinder block construction. "Brighter than the junior associate that law firm sent."

"Probably better than someone local."

"You didn't meet the out-of-town talent. He had on a corduroy jacket with leather patches on the elbows, hiking boots, and his haircut was so close he needed a Band-Aid on his scalp."

"Still, there's something to be said for being from out of town, not aware of every little indiscretion and not apt to have done anything local someone might hold over your head." Lenore brought out a salad she'd made earlier, divided the greens between two small salad plates and drizzled them with vinaigrette. She stood at one side of the island, and we both began spearing lettuce. "Our busiest local attorney is still local because of something up at the school he was involved with several years ago."

"How bad could it have been?" Small-town problems weren't really problems to outsiders until they'd made the evening news. What Lenore alluded to was ancient history to me.

"Several years ago, before you came here, we had a scandal. One of the coaches cut a little peephole in the girls' locker room. He'd rigged a camera to take pictures of them when he wasn't looking through it." Lenore paused to take a sip of her wine.

"And he put the pictures on the Internet?" I whispered.

"No. The Internet hadn't become the octopus that dominates our lives, but some of the pictures got out. I suspect one of his student aides found them not too well hidden in his desk drawer and passed them around. I never saw them, but from reports, it wasn't too difficult to tell who was who." Lenore's tone was hard, but the hardness hid a deep, soft connection to the victimized girls. I knew she didn't have a daughter of her own, but the way she spoke told me there must have been a student who was dear to her involved in the sordid business she was telling me.

"And the attorney we're speaking of?" I hoped for a name, but she didn't offer one.

"He defended one of those coaches who knew all along but didn't do anything to protect the girls."

"Why would he stay here? I'd imagine there are plenty of hard feelings on both sides."

"Too young, too stubborn, and too dependent on his family. I think it's a lack of backbone and too much ancestor worship. On his own, in a bigger town, he'd have to start over where no one knows how important his daddy is, but might remember his part in the locker-room trials. He'd be up at bat with two strikes against him to start."

"The Slaytons are new enough they don't know the story, so that can't be why they brought in someone from away." I paused to take a sip of the Chardonnay. "I guess Ginny's family has enough money and power back home they didn't even need to look into retaining someone local. I'm kind of curious about Richard Murray."

"How so?"

"Chris told me about the conflicts his dad had with other faculty, and Murray didn't seem that interested."

"Conflicts? Was my name on the list?"

I shook my head. "No. Chris mentioned Bart, and Coach Keener, and Libby."

"I had no idea Keener and Slayton weren't happy with each other."

"Chris couldn't tell me what the conflict was, but they were having very harsh words at rehearsal that day. When I told Murray, he didn't seem to care."

"He doesn't sound as attractive as Mac." Lenore said. She took a roasting pan out of the stove and filled two plates with cumin-spiced chicken and carrots.

I accepted the plate and ignored her comment about Mac. "I'm curious about Libby, too. She said she'd go see Chris with me, but she never showed."

Lenore rolled her eyes. "Libby was a scandal when she moved here."

"Our Libby? Who would have problems with Libby?" Other than the colonel, I thought.

"When Libby started teaching here, this town had never seen anything like her. The word *hippie* was still on a lot of local lips. People were suspicious of her at the time."

"Hippie is still a good enough description. How did she end up here? I mean, it's odd enough to have a history teacher who isn't a coach, but almost everyone up there at the school has some kind of connection to the community."

"Except you," Lenore pointed out.

I *was* an oddity at Quanah High. Most of the faculty had graduated from the school or at least had family ties that had brought them to town. I had grown up south of Tulsa, in Bixby.

Lenore was not a native, but Will was, and when he decided he wanted to start his contracting business in the area, she started teaching close to home. I came to Quanah with mercenary motives. My need for a job coincided with Quanah's need for a teacher. When I interviewed, the principal warned me the district rarely hired first-year teachers, and tried, in subtle ways, to find out who my people were. He hired me despite the fact I was a carpetbagger from Bixby.

"You know what they say; close only counts in horseshoes and hand grenades. Some people grumbled about you being hired too."

I didn't want to know from whom or about what, so I tried to redirect the conversation to Libby. "The suspicions about Libby couldn't have been too bad. She's still here."

"We've all accepted her as our local eccentric. I think she dresses like she pulled her clothes out of a communal pile in the morning, but kids leave her class chattering about history in a way I never see anywhere else," Lenore said. "They walk out of her room excited. They walk out of Broward's like they're headed out on the Bataan Death March."

I nodded. Broward taught history next door to Libby. Without a copying machine and a DVD player, his students would have had to satisfy themselves with trying to read the back of the newspaper Broward held in front of his face for 42 minutes of the 45-minute hour.

"And people like Libby. I can't remember the last time she had a conflict with a parent. They all seem to love her. The only person who didn't was the colonel." Lenore took our empty plates and rinsed them off in the sink.

"That seems natural, doesn't it? Here's the colonel, a spit shined stereotype of a military man, and then down the hall, Libby. The quintessential hippie." I watched her open the refrigerator and look thoughtful.

"Cheese or cheesecake for dessert?" she asked.

"You have to ask? Cheesecake!"

Lenore set the cheesecake on the counter. She took plates from the cabinet, forks from a drawer, and a small spool of dental floss from a drawer.

"Why do you have dental floss in your kitchen?" I asked.

"It's the best way to cut a cheesecake. Don't worry, it's not minty." Lenore unrolled a length of the floss, wrapped it around fingers on each hand, and cut the cake into 16 of the neatest triangles I'd ever seen.

We both took a moment to get to know the cheesecake. The smooth cream cheese tasted of dairy and citrus. The crust was barely sweet, almost bland.

"You were telling me about the conflict between Libby and the colonel," I said.

"Like you said, in some ways the differences are archetypal. But sometimes his dislike for her came across as personal, not just a cats-versus-dogs thing. His antipathy seemed out of proportion to me. They didn't know each other until he started teaching here."

"Maybe they did know each other." I paused, trying to catalog what I knew about Libby. "Where did Libby teach before Quanah?"

"I don't think she ever said." Lenore's expression mirrored mine. She took another bite of cheesecake while she thought, and said, "Odd. Every teacher will share war stories. You complain about where you are, and then you compare it to where you were. And every school has problems.

When you start teaching somewhere new, you just trade one set for another. But we don't know what problems Libby had at her last school."

"We don't know what her last school was!"

"I wonder what Carolyn could tell us about her." The school's receptionist would know anything there was to know about Libby, and would be glad to share.

"Carolyn would tell us everything she knows if we ask just right," Lenore concurred.

"I've spent more time than usual with Libby since we started working on the play, and I can't say I know much more about her. She's helped on the show. She's lent me a prop or two and some books to help with costumes." The thought of the luxurious book sidetracked me. "One of the books she gave me looks like it came out of Andrew Carnegie's personal library. The leather cover is so soft you could almost crumple it like tissue, and the endpapers have a gorgeous swirl of blues and greens. The original bookplate is in it, and everything. It's funny, but the name sounded so familiar. Elinor Huntington." I toyed with the last bit of cheesecake on my plate, but Lenore looked up sharply.

"Like the ketchup?"

"Uhm ... yeah. Are you a fan?"

"Reggie, think about it. Elinor Huntington and Elizabeth Hoffman. Does anything strike you?"

The answer was so clear even mentioning it would make me seem simple-minded. "They both have the same initials?"

"Do you know what happened to Elinor Huntington?"

117

"I guess she married a mustard mogul and they lived happily ever after."

"No. She disappeared." Lenore tapped the marble-topped island with one perfectly sculpted nail and announced, "She was involved in some environmental action out West. Or animal rescue?"

"Like trying to get people to adopt dogs?"

"No, like breaking into labs where universities and colleges were testing products on animals and setting the subjects free."

"Just letting them roam wild? She was letting defenseless animals out to fend for themselves?"

"I'm not sure of the details, I just remember there was a very intense arm of PETA that thought all animals should be free to be themselves. For them, domesticating an animal was the equivalent of slavery, and any product testing on animals was torture."

I nodded.

"But that's neither here nor there. The real question is, why does Libby have Elinor's books? Something is going on."

"Book. She gave me a book with Elinor Huntington's name in it."

Lenore looked stubborn.

"Okay, maybe two of the books had the bookplates. You've had a little too much Chardonnay and you're getting paranoid. Libby could have acquired those books in a lot of ways. She could have bought them at an estate sale, or over the Internet."

"Yes. She could have. But did she?" Lenore laid her fork down and steepled her fingers. "The birthday potluck is Monday."

"What are you going to do? Set out a bottle of Huntington's Ketchup and see if Libby gets weepy-eyed over it?"

"We'll talk to Carolyn. She can tell us about anything suspicious surrounding Libby's hiring at Quanah. And while we're at it, we can find out what was wrong between Coach Keener and the colonel. Carolyn never misses a potluck."

"With everything that's happened, do you think we'll still have it?" I'd forgotten about the lunch and hadn't been to the grocery store in over a week. I'd make a grocery run to Reasor's over the weekend and boil some eggs to devil.

"We'll sit down with Carolyn and ask some questions. I don't think it will take much to open the gates."

"And what if Libby is sitting there?"

"We'll figure it out. Asking her a couple of questions wouldn't hurt, you know. A lack of answers could reveal as much as the answers themselves."

I nodded, but I didn't agree. Lenore had invented some drama, but I thought she'd probably forget it by the time we lined up for lunch on Monday.

CHAPTER FOURTEEN

Our monthly potlucks were meant to celebrate faculty and staff birthdays, but there was an unspoken competition as well. Bring something unusual enough for people to ask for the recipe, but familiar enough the bowl it came in would go home empty. I had already conceded victory in the first race by bringing my perennial offering, but I could still grab the Miss Popularity title.

Everyone loved deviled eggs, but just like in the Miss America contest, packaging mattered. A stylist from the Food Network couldn't have plated them more fetchingly. I tucked lettuce leaves among the eggs and sprinkled paprika across the yellow yolks. I just needed the right placement among the other salads.

I didn't move fast enough.

My deviled eggs ended up right by Lenore's coleslaw.

Most of the offerings were in Pyrex. A food historian could have traced the history of that venerable company by the colors and patterns on parade. Pale celadon green and turquoise bowls from the '50s butted up against an earthy brown casserole with a mushroom motif from the '70s. My own deviled egg plate was adorable, with its pink striped edge, but Lenore's salad was in Mikasa. I had bought the eggs for my dish from the Dollar General in Quanah. I could tell some of the other cooks had used the store as a pantry for their creations as well. Beryl, our biology teacher, had brought her fruit salad cake, and I knew for a fact the canned stuff had been on sale two for a dollar last week, and the cake mixes the week before. Lenore had bought a bitter greens mix at Sprouts in Owasso. She wasn't a snob about such things, but she had standards she wasn't willing to compromise. Even for a teachers' potluck.

"Are you trying to show us up again? Is that china some of your mama's?" Beryl asked as she cut her cake into squares for serving.

"No, it's someone else's mama's. I bought a service for eight at an estate sale." Lenore smiled, and Beryl backed away.

Everyone, from support staff and faculty to the superintendent, lined up. From the back of the line, I tried to see if any of my eggs were gone. I saw our superintendent, Walter Johnson, pick up two halves. Bart did the same.

"We need to stake out a spot beside Carolyn," I whispered to Lenore, picking up a foam plate and plastic fork when the line moved forward. We both took a few spoonfuls of the dishes closest to us. I added a slice of brisket the AG teacher had cooked in the smoker built by the boys in his welding classes. I was so distracted by our mission, I ended up with pea salad on my plate. I hated the stuff. The green peas, cubes of processed cheese, and sweet salad dressing filled about a fourth of my plate.

"We're lucky she's not the life of the party." Lenore said.

Carolyn's skill at acquiring information made her less than desirable as a lunch partner. We weren't surprised to find an empty chair on either side of her when we reached the end of the line. We walked to Carolyn's table and settled down beside her with our plates.

"Carolyn, you look wonderful! Have you done something new to your hair?" My opening gambit might have made other women suspicious, but Carolyn assumed everyone would admire her architectural wonder of a hairdo.

"I went to Tawnette's as usual Saturday, but I asked her for something a little special. Earl and me have plans for Valentine's Day." Carolyn used both hands to pat her hair, which was the same poufy cotton ball of a do she always wore, only more so.

"Is it the color?" Lenore asked.

Carolyn looked over both shoulders before leaning in to confide, "Yes, I wanted a little more strawberry and a little less blond. The new girl Tawnette has working on color is a genius. The shade came out just exactly like I'd seen it in my head."

I tried to hide my shudder. Carolyn's hair was pink. Fashion-doll convertible pink. The pink that got Frenchie kicked out of beauty school in *Grease*.

Lenore and I picked at our food, neither one of us quite sure how to get Carolyn talking before Libby showed up for the potluck.

"How long have you and Earl been together, Carolyn?" Lenore's question would get Carolyn talking, but not about Libby.

"We're celebrating our fourth Valentine's Day. You know, it's the third time around for both of us." We knew. Everyone knew. Carolyn's first marriage, to a high school sweetheart, had ended so noisily the tabloid television show *A Current Affair* covered the story. Even I knew about her first marriage, and I had been in high school when the video cameras captured all the mayhem on video. Carolyn's second dissolution had been quieter, only because the man involved hadn't had enough backbone to face the cameras. He'd slipped out quietly about the time I'd moved to Quanah, and Carolyn was close-lipped about the particulars. No one could fault her judgment. She could be selective about what she'd share. Your secrets? Sure. Her secrets? Never.

"Your fourth? St. Valentine is looking out for you two, isn't he?" Lenore punctuated her comment with a sip of ice tea and then said, "I feel so sorry for people who don't have anyone to share the day with."

I frowned, but Lenore's expression told me she knew what she was doing. I let her take the lead.

"Earl and me feel the same way. Is Will planning a night on the town for you two?"

Lenore let her head droop. "No, he's back East right now. I suppose Reggie and I are going to celebrate Valentine's Day with each other. Just two old maids."

"I got a plant from one of the freshmen!" I volunteered.

"That's sad, just so sad." Carolyn shook her head.

The plant was a nice, healthy philodendron. I planned to name him. Phil, of course. But as I watched pity creep into Carolyn's eyes, I changed my mind.

"I feel for you. Before I had Earl," Carolyn said as she reached across the table to pat my hand, "I hated Valentine's Day. I'd buy my own chocolate and eat it all, just eat it all at once, on February 14. I'd be sick as a dog the next day, and then I'd be even more depressed because I didn't have no one to take care of me."

"It's not a crime or anything to not have a—" I started to say, but Lenore kicked at my ankle under the table and I quit talking. The plastic fork wasn't sturdy enough to stab the brisket on my plate in anger, so I just fumed a little.

Lenore said, "Reggie and I were just talking about whether we might persuade Libby to join us in a little celebration, but I haven't seen her today." Lenore's conversation had finally moved on to our original target. But could Carolyn track it? My grandpa always told me just because you had the bird in sight didn't mean the dog did too.

"Poor soul. She's one of the loneliest people I believe I know any day of the year, let alone Valentine's Day."

Yes! Carolyn's comment left an opening for Lenore to pursue. We might come home with a prize this time.

"I've always had that impression," Lenore agreed.

"You remember when she first got hired," Carolyn half-whispered to Lenore, "it was the oddest thing. She'd just come out of nowhere, and then there she was, hired to teach right here at Quanah."

"I didn't have much chance to know her when she first came, since she taught on one end of the building and my classroom was on the other." Lenore fed Carolyn some more conversational rope. Too much curiosity and Carolyn might shut down. Too little, and she wouldn't feel we appreciated the information.

"It wasn't a matter of knowing her. I had to put her personnel file together! Her folder had precious little in it."

"Enough to hire her, apparently," I said.

Carolyn hung on to my statement like a bird dog with the prize in his jaws. "Well, that's what's so strange. You know, before Bart was principal, you remember, Charlie Howell acted as principal and superintendent."

I looked surprised.

"The district was so small then," Carolyn exclaimed. "He hired Libby, but I can't say why. People wondered about a lot of the stuff Howell did."

"You're not saying she's unqualified, are you, Carolyn?" I may have sounded a little sharper than I meant to, and Carolyn drew back.

"If I thought something like that, I would have spoke up! She has a teaching certificate, same as you, but I remember something odd about her college transcript." Carolyn tapped her fork on her empty plate, thinking. "I haven't had any call to check on her file in so long, I can't remember just what it was. The name, I think."

"It's not her name?" I tried to sound casual.

"Of course it's her name! She's not teaching under an alias." Carolyn stood, cleaning up the litter from her lunch. "I have to get back to the office. Could one of you bring me a little sliver of the birthday cake? I hate to miss it, but I need to let Lacey go to lunch. She's covering the phones."

"Of course! Reggie and I will make sure you get a piece." Lenore's voice was cool and polite. We both watched with blank faces as Carolyn left the lounge.

Lenore and I had time to whisper together before Bart stood up to stutter through his usual birthday spiel.

"That sounded suspicious," I said.

"The cake? A lot of people won't eat sweets in public because they think it'll make them look bad," Lenore answered.

"No, I mean what she said about Libby's name. Doesn't that business about her transcript sound strange to you?"

"Vague. It sounds vague. Carolyn can be a drama queen. You don't know if it's really suspicious or not." Lenore glanced at Bart long enough to make sure he was more interested in his conversation with the superintendent than the two of us. "Keep your voice down."

"You thought the books Libby gave me were suspicious, and you don't think a problem with her personnel file could point to something odd? Wasn't it your idea to pump Carolyn for information?" I suspected Lenore's passion for detecting might decrease as her sobriety increased. Last night's Chardonnay buzz was gone, and she was being rational.

"There aren't any sides, only truth and untruth. Before we do anything else, we need to know some more." Lenore *was* interested in following up on Carolyn's comments. Maybe it wasn't just the Chardonnay. "We didn't ask her about Keener's conflict with the colonel."

"Mac's a professional. We should talk to him and let him take the next step."

"What kind of amateur sleuth are you? Whoever says, 'Oh, Mr. Sheriff, please look into this, I'll just leave it all in your hands'?"

"Every sane person even remotely involved in a murder investigation." I never reacted well to teasing. "We're not in the middle of a mystery novel, and despite your gray hair, you are not Miss Marple. I'll just let Mac know he should look into this thing with Libby."

"And he'll pat you on the head and ignore it," Lenore said. "You need to find out what Carolyn thought was so suspicious so you'll have more to share with Mac. The more facts you have, the more serious he'll take you."

"Why me?"

"You are at the center of a murder investigation, whether you want to admit it or not. The colonel was killed backstage at your play. Chris was your lead. Libby is providing props and costume advice.

Unless you can prove someone else killed the colonel, you might be the next person Mac decides to check out?"

"I wouldn't mind Mac checking me out."

"Have you thought that they might close down the auditorium if they can't figure out who did it? And then where would you do your plays?"

Lenore's words hit me like a punch in the throat. I couldn't catch my breath to respond.

"You know what I'm saying is true. You've got to act on what information we have. What we know is telling us we need to know more." Lenore's soft voice was firm and maternal.

Before she could say anything else, Bart stood up at the front of the room and began to speak. He sounded like an adult from a Charlie Brown cartoon. None of his words registered. The question, "How do I find out who Libby is?" rotated in my mind like a screen saver, tumbling and tumbling. Unlike the text on my classroom computer, the words I saw repeat in an endless loop were the dark red of fresh blood spilled on the backstage floor.

CHAPTER FIFTEEN

"Have you been backstage, Rick?" I asked the stage manager when we met in the auditorium after school. When I got permission to take the students back to the auditorium, I felt as though we were going home. Rick and I were the first ones into the space, and each cast or crew member high-fived one of us as they entered the place we all thought of as home. I reminded them to stay out front or on stage, away from the crime scene in the wings.

"It looks about the same. There wasn't anything gross."

"So we're back to normal."

"I don't think there's anything normal about putting on a play at a crime scene, but yeah, we're back where we belong, so I guess that's good," Rick said.

The release I usually felt at rehearsal wasn't there Monday afternoon. I slumped in my seat in the darkened theater and watched students run through the play, but I asked to see the same scene over and over. The repetition deadened the scene, and the actors lost energy, delivering lines in monotone.

I had more baggage to carry out to my car than a camel on a trans-Saharan trek. I wore my everyday purse, pared down to school-day essentials yet still overstuffed, like a bandolier. Over one shoulder was my ubiquitous bag of grading, crowded with essays from my English class and speech outlines from public speaking. In one hand I had a paper bag from Reasor's supermarket with my dirty deviled egg plate and a foil-wrapped package of brisket. Helen had forced the meat on me because "we single girls just don't cook enough for ourselves." In the other hand, I grasped a yellow plastic bag from Dollar General, bulging with a typical teacher's haul from the holiday. Students had left cards and little boxes of candy on my desk all day.

Balancing my load, I trudged up the aisle toward the exit. Rick had turned off all the lights onstage and backstage. The house remained lit, but the light didn't fill the space the way actors did. I felt hyper-aware of being alone in the 1200-seat space. I only needed to use my key to turn off the houselights as I left. I tried to turn it in the slot by the exit without unburdening myself, but I couldn't manage. I had to unload everything except my purse to insert the key and turn it to the right. With the light off, I fumbled around for my packages in the dark, balanced everything again, and started to lean back into the door to push my way into the glass-walled foyer.

Leaning didn't budge the door.

That was odd.

I shrugged my load back into place and moved to my right to try the door in the middle. The door opened when I leaned into it. Before I could step into the glass-lined lobby, someone lunged at me, knocking me to the floor and racing out the doors to the front foyer.

I landed hard on my hip, the door banging into my head. It continued to bounce slowly off my cranium as I tried to right myself. I wasn't moving fast enough to catch the attacker. Struggling to stand up, I had to spread my feet apart to maintain my balance as my head throbbed and my eyes watered.

Squeezing my eyes shut, I tried to remember what the intruder looked like. Whoever it was that shoved me, he or she had chosen an outfit that defied gender clues. The bulky sweatshirt, a black ski mask, dark blue jeans, and grey sneakers made up a genderless uniform, and the only really puzzling thing was the ski mask. It seemed oddly professional and out of place.

It would take me a few minutes to gather everything up, and even though the brisket had been tossed onto the carpet, I didn't feel safe enough to stay in the auditorium by myself. Bending over gave me an unpleasant head rush, so I left my stuff piled on the floor and ran to the front office. I locked the door behind me and grabbed the phone on the counter to dial the sheriff.

My head ached from the door banging into it, and my vision was blurry. Slowly, my eyes adjusted to the dim light, but when they did, I saw a strange lump behind the counter.

"Sheriff's Office."

"Mac, this is Reggie." I tried to identify the pile on the floor. It looked as though someone had dumped some clothes there, maybe some lost-and-found items from a classroom, but Carolyn would never have left such a mess at the end of the day. "Someone pushed me down as I was leaving the auditorium."

"Reggie, girl, I'd love to talk but we're hip-deep in a crisis here." Someone was shouting behind him. I couldn't make out what they were saying.

"I'm calling about a crisis." I raised my voice so Mac could hear me over the racket in his office.

His response rolled over my words like a semi rolls over an armadillo, "We've got a missing person, we think. Earl's up here telling me he can't find his sweet Carolyn."

Suddenly I made sense of the pile of clothes in front of me. I gulped and choked on the air as I realized what the pile really was.

"Reggie, really. I'll talk to you later, hon." Mac's tacking on that endearment would normally send a shiver down my spine, but I was shivering for entirely different reasons. The pain from the blow to my head and the adrenaline still pumping through my body made it difficult to form the words.

"I think I can tell you where she is, Mac."

We stopped wasting time on words, and Mac went into action. I knew I had to wait for him, but I wasn't going to wait in the same room as Carolyn. I let myself out of the office. I turned slowly in a tight circle, watching my own back, and then decided I would feel better waiting outside, under the streetlights in front of the school. It was only a few minutes until Mac pulled up in his official Chevy Yukon with the county seal on the doors.

Mac pulled in to the curb, parked askew, and was barely out of the SUV when he started talking. "What are you doing out here? There might be someone hanging around meaning to do you some harm." He covered the space between us in long strides, and put his glove-covered hands on my shoulders. My coat was still on the floor by the auditorium doors, and I was shivering in the night air.

"They already got Carolyn." Pulling me close, Mac led me to the front doors of the school and inside, where it was only marginally warmer.

"Slow down and tell me everything."

I had to shake my head a little, trying to organize my thoughts. Did I need to tell him about the intruder in the auditorium first? Or should I tell him about Carolyn?

An ambulance blared into the parking lot and the same paramedics who had come for the colonel swept by us at Mac's signal and into the office. Right behind them was our principal, Bart, and then Shrimp.

"Sheriff, what is it? Has someone set off that alarm again? If I can catch those kids, it'll be the last time they use the school for one of their hooligan pranks." Bart looked more casual than I'd ever seen him, which meant he wore the same short-sleeved dress shirt he wore day in and day out, the same neatly pressed but generic dress pants, but had skipped the tie.

"I don't guess I was clear enough on the phone about what's going on, Bart. We've had another incident here."

"We'll be looking into it, Mr. Lincoln," Shrimp said. "Don't worry. First, I'm sure we'll be asking Ms. Murphy here a few questions. Has Mac advised you of your rights?" Shrimp had stretched to his maximum height as he delivered the official-sounding comments to Bart, but Mac cut him back down a notch.

"Shrimp, I don't think we'll need to advise Ms. Murphy of anything. She's had a bit of a shock."

"But Sheriff, she's the common denominator."

"Do you have any idea what's going on here? We've both just arrived, and we don't know what we've got on our hands." Mac was sharp, and Shrimp faded back, but he wouldn't quit looking at me, and his hand rested lightly on the pistol on his belt.

"If you don't know what's going on yet, why did you call me?" Bart snapped.

"I knew we'd need someone responsible here, and you're the administrator that lives closest. Let me see what the paramedics have to say, and we'll sort all this out."

Mac moved into the office, leaving the three of us in the foyer looking at one another.

Bart broke the silence. "Reggie, what were you doing up here? It's Valentine's Day. Didn't you have anywhere better to be?" Bart was trying to blame me for ruining his evening. I didn't have much sympathy, as he was not the one who'd found Carolyn. I tried to retort, but Shrimp interrupted.

"I'm sure Mac won't want the two of you discussing anything until after he's questioned ... I mean, talked to you both. Let's just hold our peace for now." Shrimp still had his hand resting on his service revolver, and although he spoke to Bart, his narrow gaze was trained on me.

I didn't feel coherent enough to have a conversation anyway. The combination of tension, fear, and low blood sugar made me feel teary and whiny. I wrapped my arms around myself for some extra warmth and kept my eyes focused on the floor until Mac returned.

"There's no good news, y'all. Carolyn's dead." I choked a little at that, even though it wasn't really news. Carolyn was a gossip, and a little vain about that awful hair, but she was so goodhearted.

"Do you think it was murder?" Bart asked.

"We can't tell right now. We'll need to seal off the office so we can do our looking around. You and Reggie can head on home, I guess."

Shrimp started to say something, and then stopped himself.

"I should probably stay here, Sheriff. Can I at least go in there to call our superintendent?" Bart asked.

"You don't want to go in there, Bart. Go use one of the classroom phones. I'll walk Ms. Murphy out to her car while you do that." Mac took my elbow and led me out the front door.

"I don't have my purse or anything," I said woodenly, searching through my pockets for my car keys, "it's all in the auditorium where that person tried to attack me."

"Someone tried to attack you?"

"That's why I called you in the first place. I was leaving rehearsal, and out of nowhere, someone pushed me into the exit doors and then ran away."

"Well, that may be the same person who got Carolyn. I was going to send you on home, but now I'm not so sure you'll be alright by yourself." Mac had one hand on my bicep and stood, weighing his options.

I wasn't that sure, either, but I didn't let Mac know. "I can call Lenore to come over or spend the night with her. Will's out of town, and she'd welcome some company."

Mac tilted his head, thinking, and said, "That sounds good. I'll check on you when we finish up here. Bring your stuff from the auditorium. It'll be late, though."

"I'm a night owl."

"Go straight home. No sightseeing." Mac teasingly shook a finger at me.

"Cross my heart and hope to ..." I couldn't finish that sentence because I was suddenly sobbing. Mac gathered me up in his arms and let me cry into his chest. I shuddered and wept for a long time.

"It's all catching up to you. You'll be alright." He didn't seem annoyed at the tears, the way so many men do, and he didn't try to tease me out of them. He was just matter-of-fact, and that made me feel brave again. "Get on home."

He headed back for the front doors of the school, but he stood and watched me pull out onto the highway and head for home before he went inside.

CHAPTER SIXTEEN

Instead of keeping my promise to Mac to call Lenore when I got home, I changed into my pajamas and sat down at my computer to check my e-mail.

After I'd made sure Gus's bowl was filled.

He watched me deposit a scant cupful of dry food into his metal dish and top it with a generous spoonful of chicken and then nodded as I refilled his other bowl with fresh water. Once I'd delivered his meal, he gave his full attention to the repast, and I was dismissed.

"That's it? That's all I get?" Gus might have shrugged off my plaint, but it was more likely the movement in his shoulders indicated the speed at which he was gobbling the food. If I'd wanted affirmations, I would have adopted a dog. I left him to his dinner and headed for my computer.

My office was also my guest room and my studio for the art and craft projects that I engaged in with serial enthusiasm. Most importantly, the room was my library, with two walls of shelves filled with books I had neatly organized by category---fiction, pedagogy, drama, mystery, true crime---when I first unpacked my books. Now books stood straight on most of the shelves, but the orderly rows were almost lost behind the stacks of books in front of them. I sometimes thought to myself how lucky I was to have a book habit instead of a drug habit.

Checking my e-mail was mostly reflex. That's what I did when I walked in the door each evening. After the awful events at the school, I still felt a little shaky, but mostly I wanted to feel normal. And normal was being home alone, checking e-mail.

I shook my head at the amount of unsolicited ads cluttering my inbox, and clicked to delete the names I didn't recognize until I spotted "SocrGrl05" in the "from" column. That name sounded familiar.

SocrGrl05 was Abby. Several students had turned in work by e-mailing me papers to eke out every available minute by a deadline, and Abby was one of them. I sat down at the computer. The message came up on the screen:

Ms. Murphy:

I hope you're okay. You probably know it was me that tried to scare you in the auditorium tonight.

No, Abby hadn't been on my list of possibilities. I felt a tingle of apprehension as I thought about Carolyn. Had Abby been in the front office as well?

I don't know what I was thinking. I just wanted you to feel scared and helpless like I do. You've always been my favorite teacher and when you didn't give me Juliet, I got really mad. And then you found out I'd copied all that for my paper and I knew you couldn't stand me anymore. Attacking you tonight wasn't right. It wasn't even equal. Paybacks, I mean.

I'm sorry.

I hope you can forgive me.

Please don't tell my parents.

She was worried about what her parents would think. I had tried to be empathetic, but this escapade had drained me of any sympathy for Abby. More than that, I was frightened. What if Abby had attacked Carolyn? As fast as I had left the auditorium after being shoved into the door, the intruder couldn't have gone to Carolyn after she pushed me. But Abby could have encountered Carolyn first.

I looked back at the message and finished reading it.

I saw Ms. Hoffman leaving when I ran out of the auditorium. Don't think I'm telling you that just to keep her from tattling on me. I heard about what happened to Carolyn and I'm scared. I knew someone has to know what I saw and I thought I could tell you.

If you're not still mad.

Most days when I let rehearsal out early, the basketball team was still practicing in the gym, which opened off the same lobby as the auditorium. Tonight, however, Coach Lawrence and the boys had gone to a tournament at Mustang, so the gym and lobby were both deserted. The classroom area was removed from the lobby and front office. If an intruder had been both in the front office and the auditorium, he or she could have gone from one to another without being noticed. The night custodians were usually in the classrooms cleaning at that time.

But if it had been Abby in both places, how did she get in? She hadn't been called for rehearsal that day, and the front doors were locked at 3:15. The doors to the classroom area were locked soon after, so the only way into the building was with a key.

I minimized my e-mail and opened a new document. Typing as quickly as I could, I tried to create a time line:

2:45. Last bell.

School was out, and the hordes of teenagers who had been held captive were loosed to plunder lockers and race out to their cars or amble to the curb where the buses would pick them up to deliver home.

3:15 Front doors locked. Doors to classroom area locked.

I usually wandered by the front doors on my way to unlock the auditorium for rehearsal. Once the doors between the classrooms and the front foyer were locked, cast and crew had to go through the gym without getting hit by a practice ball or yelled at by Coach Lawrence for walking on the gym floor in street shoes.

Everyone who needed to be at rehearsal had been there. Physically. None of us had made it mentally.

3:30 Carolyn leaves for home.

But not today.

5:00 I dismissed everyone from rehearsal.

After everyone left, I took another few minutes to gather the pile of stuff I'd dropped at the door of the auditorium. By the time I'd turned off the lights, been attacked, and made my way to the office, it was dark outside and close to 5:30.

What was this time line supposed to tell me?

Maybe Abby did have time to dart to the front office. But just as I couldn't imagine Chris as a murderer, I couldn't imagine Abby as one either, even though she'd shoved me into those doors.

A knock at my front door startled me out of my own world.

"Reggie, are you home?" It was Mac. That voice was unmistakable, not just because of the tone but because of the uncontrollable physiological response I had to it.

"Just a minute!" I grabbed a robe and put it on, opening the door as soon as I could.

"It's still frosty out here, Reggie. Are you going to let me come in where it's warm or just admire me framed in your doorway?" Mac grinned, and I realized that I had been staring at him. I hoped it hadn't been a slack-jawed stare.

"Come in, Sheriff."

"This is only partly official business. I think you can keep calling me Mac." He peeled off the lined denim jacket he wore without being asked, and tossed it, along with his hat, on a handy chair.

"Do you want something to warm you up?"

"Got any sippin' whiskey?"

"Aren't you still on duty or something? Can you do that?"

"I was just teasing, Reg."

Either my sense of humor had been deactivated by the evening's events or hormones were making me stupid. "I meant would you like some tea or hot chocolate?"

"Hook me up with that chocolate."

Mac followed me into the kitchen, where I filled the kettle again and put it back on the stove. I broke out another mug and opened two packs of hot chocolate, shaking them into the cups to await the boiling water. Mac just leaned against the counter and watched.

"Well?" I prodded him. I was very curious about what had happened after I'd left the school.

"It's pretty clear it's another homicide."

"That's terrible! Here, in Quanah." The news wasn't news to me. I'd seen Carolyn sprawled in the office.

"You're an English teacher, you've heard that stuff about death not being a respecter of persons."

"I've heard that, but it's more that crimes like these always seem to happen somewhere else. I don't think any of us are prepared when it happens here."

"Crimes like these? Oh, this and the colonel. I'm not sure there's a connection."

"Come on," I said as I poured the water into the cups and stirred the powder and liquid into something rich and chocolate. "No homicides in Quanah for decades, and then two in one week? There has to be a connection."

Mac nodded.

I thought about the possibility of the two murders being committed by the same person, and my face relaxed a little. Mac noticed. "What light bulb went on in your head?"

"Does this mean Chris isn't a suspect?"

"It may. The fingerprints on the murder weapon we had in the colonel's case don't belong to Chris."

"It may? If the fingerprints aren't his on the weapon involved in the colonel's murder, and he's sitting in jail tonight as Carolyn is murdered, that seems to pretty well clear him." I had slammed my cup of hot chocolate down on the counter at Mac's refusal to admit that Chris was cleared. The hot drink splashed out on my hand, and I had to hold it under cold water to take the sting out.

Mac moved next to me and took my hand, turning it underneath the cold water. My hand was cooling off, but everything else seemed to be heating up.

"Chris is probably not our man." Mac picked up the dishcloth from the counter and wrapped my hand with it. "For the murder. But he showed up at school with a backpack full of spray paint."

"He didn't do anything with them. You and Shrimp had him handcuffed and on the way to a cell before anyone could say boo."

Mac was silent, nodding. "That's fair. I'm not a man to say everything I'm thinking, and it's habit to keep all the details of an investigation close so I don't mess it up."

"So you don't think Chris did it?"

"Like I said, he's probably not our man."

"It may not be a man at all. I know who pushed me around tonight, Mac."

He only raised his eyebrows and waited.

"Abby Beamer. She e-mailed me an apology."

He nodded, and I could almost see him trying to match Abby with the crime scene in the high school

143

office. His mental processes were so transparent. I watched how his face moved as he tried out various ideas. I hope he didn't play much poker.

"Mac, it couldn't have been Abby."

"I think you need to leave that kind of decision to me, Reggie. I'm the professional here."

Being told what to do brought my streak of stubborn out. "Well, Mr. Professional, what if I told you that Abby saw Libby leaving the front of the school the same time she was running out of the auditorium?"

"I'd say thank you for sharing that information with the law enforcement officer investigating." Mac took a sip of the hot chocolate. "That's interesting. But remember, that's not official yet about Chris. I have few things to take care of, and then by tomorrow afternoon he'll be out of our jail. I'll be talking to Abby tomorrow too."

"So Chris is definitely off your list of suspects?"

"Probably." Mac grinned at me with that one-word answer. I thought about sharing what Lenore and I had talked about but Mac moved a little closer and I stopped thinking about the murders.

"You didn't call Lenore," he said.

"You're here to keep me safe." I moved in a little myself until we were almost touching, and I lifted my eyes just a bit so I could look straight into his.

"But I can't stay. You're lovely, Reggie. And I want to get to know you. But not like this, when we're both distracted by the stuff that's happening around us. You're practically at the center of all this. I can't be carrying on with you right now."

"You're not scared of Shrimp, are you?"

His laugh was bigger than he was, rocking him back on his heels. Being so close to him was like touching my tongue to a nine-volt battery, but his laugh could start a car.

"I am not afraid of Shrimp Standfield. And don't you be." He looked around the kitchen, the deadbolt on the door that led outside, the shades pulled, and then said, "You look like you'll be okay here. I don't think you really need Lenore to protect you. I've got to be going, though."

So he did.

I saw him out the front door, skipping the kiss I wanted to steal from him, as anyone passing by might have seen the sheriff kissing the schoolteacher and that would not have been good for either of us.

CHAPTER SEVENTEEN

When I woke the next morning the light outside was flat and gray. The whole world looked like an overexposed snapshot of my childhood. My mind wasn't as static as the world outside though, and as I got ready to go, I made a list of what I needed to do. Little of it had anything to do with teaching.

Pick up what I'd left in the auditorium when I rushed out last night.

Check up on Libby.

Find out what the colonel and Coach Keener were arguing about.

Lenore and I planned to have dinner at her place again since Will was on another trip, so we could compare notes if we didn't run into each other at school.

Mac didn't want me to do any investigating, but I couldn't quell my curiosity. When the murderer invaded our rehearsal, he or she had made it my business to find out their identity. Besides, I had given Mac some important information along the way. He should be grateful he had someone inside the school to help flesh out his inquiry.

Once in my classroom, I booted up my computer and got online.

I had to find out something about Libby.

When I searched *Libby Hoffman*, all I found were a couple of articles from our local paper about school activities she'd been involved in. Plugging in her name with some other terms brought nothing. I tried a basic search on some genealogy sites, but when the name or its variants popped up, it usually belonged to someone else. Frustrated by the lack of results, I had to admit a search for my name would probably be just as fruitless.

Before I logged off, I typed *Elinor Huntington* into the search engine. Over a million results popped up. One led to a website devoted to unsolved crimes. I followed the link and found an article headed "Huntington, Elinor." While there were no pictures, I was riveted by the prose. Scrolling down, I read how Elinor had come from a very wealthy family whose fortunes were tied to the production of America's favorite condiment. In some ways, her story was reminiscent of Gloria Vanderbilt or Patty Hearst. Her life was an arc that paralleled the lonely childhood Gloria had had, and then met the diminishing arc of Patty's revolutionary period. It was eerie how closely Elinor's involvement with extreme environmentalist elements paralleled Patty's journey with the Symbionese Liberation Army in the early 1970s. But while Patty was rescued from her "consciousness raising," Elinor simply disappeared.

The article told me a radical environmentalist group Elinor was part of had been linked to an explosion in a university laboratory in Arkansas thirty years ago. When the group threatened to blow up the lab, the chancellor had posted ROTC cadets from the school to guard the building after the scientists moved animals to a safe place. The group still managed to plant an incendiary device and when it went off, several cadets were injured and one was killed. Elinor was about to go on trial with others from the group when she disappeared.

The warning bell distracted me, and I looked at the clock. I only had five minutes to get ready for the first wave of students. A couple of dozen made it into their seats before the tardy bell, and one slid into his seat just before I could shut the door behind them.

Passing back papers, I overheard Danny Johnson complaining.

"I sure hated to see the colonel get taken out," he confided to the kid across the row from him. Instead of reminding him to get back to his ten-minute writing, I listened. Danny was the star wrestler Lenore and I had discussed over dinner a few nights before. Maybe Danny's complaint would illuminate the conflict between the math teacher and the wrestling coach.

To his credit, Josh, the kid Danny spoke to, continued writing and just shrugged. Danny took the minimal response as encouragement to keep talking.

"Coach has really come down on me hard. He knew my math grade was crap, and now he's taking it out on me at practice."

"What does that have to do with the colonel?" Josh asked. I was glad, since I didn't understand the connection either, but I didn't want to bust in on their conversation.

"The colonel was sending me to detention every day instead of practice. Coach didn't like that, but there wasn't anything he could do. I mean, I guess he talked to the colonel or something, but the colonel told me unless I had a C in his class, I was being insubordinate and belonged in the stockade. I thought I'd be okay with the colonel gone, but it's tearing me up. The sub doesn't care if I've got a D, but Coach has his foot up my butt every day."

"I guess detention wasn't as hard, huh?"

"I don't need all that intensity. I'm the best wrestler they've got on the team."

I'd heard enough to process how Danny's plight connected with the argument between the colonel and Coach Keener. Keener resented Slayton sending Danny to detention every day, making the boy miss practice. The wrestling coach wanted to know his boys were behaving in class, and if they weren't, he'd be on top of them. Overhearing Danny gave me some context for the argument I'd heard between the two men at rehearsal that day. What would Keener say if I talked to him?

I had a chance to find out between classes. I took my mug and went to the front office to get some coffee. I'd run into Keener doing the same about that time on other days, so it was worth the chance. Crossing the commons in the center of the building, I passed Libby.

"Hey, I found a picture you might want back in

one of those books you gave me," I said, not meaning to detain her or slow my progress to the front office. "I'll send it down with a student next hour."

"A picture?" Libby stopped.

"It's a glossy print of some kind of protest. I wasn't sure if you needed it for anything you're doing right now, but sorry I forgot about it."

"Just send it down. It's not that important." Her voice cracked a little, and she turned away from me. I headed for the front office, where I hit the jackpot.

Keener was at the sink in the tiny faculty coffee lounge, filling a shaker bottle with water to dissolve the cream-colored powder resting in the bottom.

"Coach," I said.

"How we doing?"

"Pretty good. How about you?"

He shrugged. "You know how it is. Wrapping up the season in the next couple of weeks."

"Danny holding on okay?"

Keener snorted. "Yeah, he's okay. Is he doing alright in your class?"

It was my turn to make a vague gesture, so I shrugged and replied, "Oh, he's fine. He likes to talk a little too much when he should be writing, but not enough to be disruptive."

"Good. I'd had some bad reports and tried to impress on him how he should be behaving."

"I might have heard something about that."

"I didn't think ... " Keener had screwed the top back on the shaker, but he didn't look back up at me right away. "I didn't think you'd heard what we were actually saying that day."

"In the auditorium? Was that about Danny?"

"I'm sorry we caused a ruckus, Reg. I was so angry with the colonel," Keener said, and then lowered his voice so no one would overhear. "I'd asked him to tell me if he had any problems with the wrestlers, but he wouldn't. He'd been sending Danny to detention over and over instead of letting me know so I could deal with it. Danny needs the time on the mat, and every time he'd spend a few days in detention and then win another match, the whole process would just inflate his ego."

"If he was good enough to keep winning without practicing, I could see that happening."

The coach shook his head. "He wasn't. He just lucked into some pairings where he was undermatched."

"You didn't get to pursue the conversation any further with the colonel, then?"

"I headed to my own practice after I left rehearsal. You can ask the other coaches who were there. I went in a little red-faced over the talk I'd had with the colonel, but I didn't see him again." Keener looked at me closely now, his shaker bottle forgotten. "You don't think I did that, do you?"

I shook my head. "No, I don't think so. It sounds like you had a legitimate reason to be upset with him and a place to be when you left."

"Well, I guess I'm grateful I passed your test." Keener took a hesitant sip of his protein drink. "You know, the sheriff already talked to me about this. Aren't you coordinating your investigations?"

"I'm not investigating, I was just curious because, you know, I was there." I squirmed a little at Keener's comment. I *was* investigating. The colonel's murderer had struck too close to my troupe, and I wanted to know who had done it.

I ticked off the teacher tasks on my list and met students in the auditorium after school. Trying to get Lab to take Mercutio's death seriously took up an inordinate amount of our time, but I had a soft spot for the character and the kid playing him, so I left in a good mood.

Lenore was waiting at the door when I drove up to her house after rehearsal. She'd had time to shed her school clothes and donned something soft and comfortable. I was still wearing my navy suit with a pink shell.

"How was rehearsal?" she asked, leading me to the island in her kitchen and pulling a pitcher of iced tea out of the refrigerator.

"I was a bit distracted. I have so much to tell you."

"Start with why you didn't you call me last night?"

"I was okay."

"And all alone there in that house. I ought to call your mama."

"Lenore, I don't know where this mother tigress thing is coming from, but you can cut it out. I'm fine. Abby Beamer scared me a little, but I'm fine."

"Abby Beamer! What does she have to do with anything?"

"Abby gave me a scare last night when I was locking up after rehearsal. She didn't have anything to do with Carolyn."

"How did I not hear about this today?" Lenore almost dropped the green Frankoma platter she'd pulled from the cabinet. She did knock over the box of crackers already on the island, but righted them and tapped her fingernails against the concrete as she glared at me.

"I don't imagine Abby wanted to brag about knocking me down and then sending me a confession via e-mail."

Lenore shook her head. "Not her finest moment. She's had a terrible week."

I stared at her.

"She's not been herself, is all. I know other people have had a more terrible week. Do you want to give me the details?"

"It's not important. Other stuff has come up today." I took one of the crackers and spread it with the creamy dip from the bowl Lenore had set on the tray. "I told you about the colonel and Coach Keener having the argument at the rehearsal, right? I found out why they were arguing, and I'm sure Keener left after that and couldn't have gone backstage to stab the colonel."

"You're sure? What does Mac say?"

"I don't know yet. He hasn't been around to catch up on the details."

"You could call him."

"He doesn't want to hear anything from me about this investigation. I told him about the argument, and he said he'd handle it."

"So you just went ahead and questioned someone who might be a suspect anyway."

"You're worse than he is! I just confirmed that Keener had a professional difference of opinion with Slayton and that he had an alibi after he left the rehearsal. Mac will follow up on that."

"I did hear that he'd let Chris go, so what happens now?"

"I couldn't find anything about Libby when I poked around online, but I did find out more about Elinor Huntington. She vanished before she could be tried for the bombing of the laboratory. Her disappearance lines up with Libby's appearance in Quanah."

Lenore's raised her eyebrows. "How closely?"

"The same year."

"That's not a very close correlation." Lenore waved her hand to dismiss my news. "Let's switch gears. What do we know about the colonel?"

"Retired military, got his teaching certificate through an alternative process. Authoritarian in the classroom and at home." I offered a short list in response.

"What branch?"

"I don't know." I paused and tried to remember if I'd ever heard. "I'm surprised I don't know."

"You've done the work on Libby, let's see what we can find out about the colonel. Bring your tea." Lenore led me into the office she and Will shared. A low counter ran around two sides of the room. Above it on one wall was a bank of windows with no curtains. The filmy gauze draped across the rod above them allowed a full view of the neatly clipped backyard that sloped down to a dense growth of trees. In the center of this counter was Lenore's computer.

"Maybe his obituary will tell us." Lenore sat down at the computer and clicked on the browser button.

I peered over her shoulder to see the results when she went to the funeral home page and found his online visitation.

"National Guard," Lenore said.

"What? I thought he was career military."

"He was. There are full-time National Guard officers on the state and federal level. Looks like the colonel had moved up in the California Guard before he retired."

I scanned the write-up, but nothing caught my attention. The obituary was boilerplate and included a brief biography that revealed little other than whoever wrote it didn't know the colonel well. "I don't see much there. See what happens if you google him."

"Okay." Lenore typed the colonel's name into the search engine along with his rank. A list of links appeared, and she clicked on the first one, an article from *The Los Angeles Times*.

I read the title, "GOVERNOR CALLS IN GUARD TO DISMISS PROTESTORS."

"So he was a major, and his squad got deployed when this environmental group was threatening a lab on the UCLA campus." Lenore summarized what we'd both seen on the screen. "They didn't speak to him directly. I guess giving interviews on the job would be a no-no."

"What else?"

Lenore went back to the list and found another article dated a day later.

"EXPLOSIVE PROTEST ENDS IN DEATH," the headline said.

"That's a terrible headline! Using a pun like that in a story that ended in such a tragedy." Lenore tsked at the article she'd found. "I remember when that happened. Some group had actually planted a bomb, and the night the protests got so violent, it went off. The bomb killed a student who was working in the lab at the time."

I focused on a picture at the top of the screen.

"Click on the photo," I said. "I've seen that picture before."

Enlarged on the computer monitor was the picture I'd found in the book Libby had lent me. The guardsmen lined along one side, a group of protesters along the other. One of the soldiers caught my eye.

I poked Lenore's shoulder and then pointed at the screen. "Don't you recognize him?"

"Who?"

I pointed at the officer nearest the lens in the photo.

It was Slayton.

"No, it can't be. What a brush with history." Lenore squinted. "I can barely make out the name patch on his fatigues."

"I think I still have the photo. I was going to return it to Libby, but I forgot about it after I mentioned it to her today." I ran for my bag, and came back in rummaging through it for Libby's books.

"What was she doing with it?" Lenore swiveled around in the chair.

"I thought she might be using it for some unit she was teaching." I dug the book out and flipped through it. The photo was gone. "That's strange. I know I put it back."

"Maybe Libby got it?"

"I said I'd send it back to her. Why would she steal it?"

"There's something about that photo she doesn't want you to know, but given the fact that the last person we talked to her about is dead, I'm not sure I'm up for any more amateur sleuthing."

"Oh. Carolyn."

"Yes, 'Oh, Carolyn.'"

"Just look at the picture again," I said. "Does anyone else look familiar?"

"I can believe that's the colonel," Lenore replied after she'd scrutinized the photo, "but no one else stands out."

"The protesters? Could any of them be Libby?"

"Maybe." Lenore sighed. "It's not that great a picture and besides, it was a long time ago. I don't recognize her, but she might have changed her appearance considerably if she was part of that."

"Do you think we need to call the sheriff?"

"And tell him what? Aside from the two murders, there's also a federal fugitive loose in Quanah?"

"He might want a heads up."

"And he might laugh us out of the office."

"We have to let Mac know. I've got his cell number."

No answer.

I left a message for him to call back as quickly as he could.

"You stay here tonight. I don't feel safe sending you back to be by yourself." Lenore said.

"I didn't bring a thing with me."

"We'll manage."

"We don't even know if we know anything."

"Libby may have the photo, and if it's because she's in it, you may be in danger. You spending the night will make us both feel safer. We can caravan to school and stop by your place so you can get something fresh to wear before we go on in for first hour. There's safety in numbers."

CHAPTER EIGHTEEN

"My daughter would never be violent toward anyone. We've raised her better than that. I think with the happenings around here, you'd be better off looking for a real criminal." Mrs. Beamer's voice grated on me in the hot office. I sat with my hands folded in my lap, the only sign of life my foot as it tapped, tapped, tapped on the carpeted floor.

The dozen hours since Lenore and I had sat down at her computer the night before had been tense. We had formulated a theory about the two recent murders. I wanted to share it with Mac. First, though, I had to make it through this meeting. Even with a stop at my house so I could change, we timed it so we'd arrived at school just as first period started. We'd gone straight to our classrooms, trying to minimize the chance we'd run into any other faculty members, especially Libby. Before I could get started teaching, Bart had called me to the front office and sent Helen to cover my class since she had first-hour plan.

Now, when I was so close to Mac I could touch him, I had to suffer through a meeting with two recalcitrant parents and their teenage thug. Bart had barricaded himself behind his desk, as usual. The Beamers sat side by side to his right, with Abby in a chair directly behind them. Mac sat on the corner of Bart's desk.

"We're doing all we can about our recent tragedies. That's not what we're here about though. Abby attacked Ms. Murphy in the auditorium, and she will have to face the consequences," Mac said.

Mr. Beamer nodded, not in agreement, but as a scholar nods in comprehension when someone speaks. He remained silent. Mrs. Beamer did not.

"Sheriff, I'd like to know what evidence you have that our daughter had anything to do with Ms. Murphy's incident."

"I have an e-mail she sent to Reggie admitting that she was the one who shoved her out of the doors and then ran. Shortly thereafter, Ms. Murphy found the body of the school receptionist."

"You're not implying our daughter murdered someone, are you?" Mrs. Beamer scooted up in her seat with each new outrage, and I was afraid she was going to fly into Mac on the next one.

"No," he said. "What I am saying is that we know she attacked Ms. Murphy. Bart, am I stuttering?" Mac turned to the principal to make sure his meaning was clear. Even Mac's calm was beginning to ripple at Mrs. Beamer's tenacity.

"No, Sheriff. I think we understand each other."

"Anyone could have sent that e-mail," Mrs. Beamer offered.

"Abby," Mac asked gently, "did you send the e-mail?"

Abby nodded slowly, but stopped as her parents turned to measure her response.

"Don't, Abby!" Her mother turned back to the rest of the group to finish her reprimand. "You shouldn't be saying anything."

As though she could get in a word with her mother's quick responses.

Bart turned to the Beamers. "Abby needs to stay home for a few days until we get this all sorted out. You understand."

"No, I don't. You've allowed Ms. Murphy to impugn our daughter's reputation for honesty by claiming she stole a paper, and now you believe that our daughter tried to harm her. We'll be contacting our lawyers." At her nod, Mr. Beamer rose from his chair and followed his wife out of the office. Abby followed, with a small shrug and smile at me.

I didn't respond. Abby didn't scare me. More than anything, I felt pity for her and wondered how she would be able to grow into a decent human being with her mother's influence.

"Abby will be needing one," Mac called after the trio. Either his voice didn't reach them or they ignored him. The Beamers left without turning around.

"Mac, thanks for your help on this. Reggie, you need to get to class." Bart stood behind his desk and stretched.

"I do need to talk to Mac for a minute."

"I'll see you later then. We probably need to talk about how to approach this situation with Abby now that we've met with her parents." Bart sat down to pick up his phone.

Mac and I left Bart's office and crossed the lobby toward the classroom area.

"Mac, I think I know something that might help figure out just what happened to the colonel. It might have something to do with Carolyn too. I'm not sure." We continued down the hall to my room.

"What is it?"

"You know about Elinor Huntington?" I asked.

Mac nodded. "Yes. That rich girl that ran out on a murder trial. That must have been thirty years ago. I know it involved some explosion at a lab and a young man got killed."

"Elinor Huntington disappeared," I confirmed. What I had to tell Mac was farfetched, so I moved slowly.

"Yeah."

"And about the time she did, Libby Hoffman started teaching here. Everyone thought she was real unusual for Quanah. Even Carolyn seemed to remember something strange about her being hired."

Mac squinted at me and waited. He wasn't making this easy. I thought that if I laid it out logically, he'd come to the same conclusion I had.

"Mac, Libby Hoffman is Elinor Huntington."

He erupted in laughter. I loved his laugh, but I hated hearing it now.

"It's true, Mac. And there's more." I pulled the photo I'd printed off the web at Lenore's handed it to him. "The timing is right. Look at the picture. There's the colonel."

Mac took the picture and studied it. "Okay. But

what does this prove?"

"Nothing, yet, but I had a copy of that picture that I found in one of the books Libby lent me, and it disappeared yesterday."

"Uh-huh." Mac nodded, waiting for me to cut to the chase.

"I think Libby might be one of the protesters in the crowd. I think Elinor Huntington, who we know as Libby, is in that crowd somewhere, maybe even close enough to the colonel that he would recognize her."

"It's hard to make any of them out." Mac tapped each face in the picture as if he were checking them against a lineup in his head. "And if we don't recognize her, then how would the colonel?"

"We haven't been that close in that intense a situation. I think he'd remember, and if he did, what would happen if he turned her in to the Feds? Elinor Huntington is still at large. She was never tried for that murder charge."

"I'm guessing I need to talk to Libby."

"I've got a better idea. I think she'll run like a rabbit if you tell her you want to talk. Let me talk to her."

"Haven't we already decided that I'm the professional?"

"You want to know if she knew the colonel before he started teaching here, right? If you knew that much, you could take her in for questioning or suspicion of murder or something, right?"

Mac nodded.

"So let me get her to admit that. I'll get her to come meet me. In the auditorium, maybe, and you can hide out and listen. When you hear what you need, pop out and cuff her." I waited, my knuckles turning white from the tension as I grasped the arms of the chair I sat in. Would Mac trust me and let me help?

"I don't know why I can't just walk into her classroom right now and find out what I need to know. That would keep you out of it."

"You need a woman for another woman to open up."

Mac started speaking slowly, as if he wanted to make sure I absorbed every word. "You will ask her to meet you in the auditorium before practice after school today. Can you keep clear of her until then?"

I nodded.

"And can you keep from telling Lenore? I don't need another amateur on this case."

My face flushed.

"Dammit, you've already told her, haven't you?" Mac ran his hand through his hair and closed his eyes. His lips moved, but no sound came out.

"What are you doing?"

"Counting to five for patience." He took a deep breath and then spoke again. "Shrimp and I ..."

I must have grimaced a bit at the deputy's name, but Mac put up a warning hand and continued.

"Shrimp, who is a duly authorized officer of the law, unlike some people present, will conceal himself backstage with me. We will attach a wire so we can record your conversation. We will listen to your exchange. At the appropriate time, I will signal Shrimp, and we will show ourselves and make an arrest."

I nodded.

"Reggie, you must have used some kind of voodoo on me to get me to agree to do this."

"You won't regret it, Mac."

CHAPTER NINETEEN

I taught my classes and managed to evade Lenore at lunch by telling her I had a stack of copies to make in the front office. Instead, I showed Mac a couple of likely spots in the auditorium where he and Shrimp could conceal themselves. I also had to figure out how to get Libby down there, finally settling on just a plain phone call.

Right after the bell rang, I dialed her room from mine.

"Libby, I need to pick your brain. Can you meet me in the auditorium?"

I heard her hesitate, but then she said, "Sure, I'll be right down."

I didn't feel good about lying to her, but then I thought about the lie she had been living for so long. If I was right, the colonel had threatened to expose that lie, and Libby had acted to protect herself.

When Libby followed me into the auditorium, I

was standing at the stage, spreading out two dresses that I was considering for Juliet.

"What's up, Reggie? How are the costumes coming?" Libby started speaking as she walked down the aisle toward me, but her faint voice made it difficult to hear her well. If I couldn't hear her, I knew Mac and Shrimp wouldn't backstage. She was ready to go home. I could tell because of the enormous tote bag she had slung over one shoulder.

"I'm sorry, what did you say? I must have zoned out." I was distracted by the thought of what she might be hiding in her bag. I was grateful Mac and Shrimp were just out of sight backstage, but if she had another sharp object, they might not be able to come to my aid in time.

"Just wondering why you need me. Are the costumes okay?"

"I wanted you to look at these and tell me what you think." I turned back to the dresses. Libby stepped up beside me and looked seriously at each dress. I tried to sound casual and remarked, "Losing Carolyn has really set people reeling around here."

"Uh-huh." Libby was focused on the little details of the dresses in front of us. She set her bag on the lip of the stage beside them, and gathered the material of one dress in her hands, kneading it like a kitten kneads its mother before nursing.

"I don't know when we'll all get back to normal."

"No." Libby nodded, her hands still working at the material.

"It's always hard to say goodbye to old friends."

Libby snorted. "Carolyn was a busybody. Knew everything and told most."

Her change in tone made me back up. I had to get her talking about the colonel, but she wouldn't believe I was missing him, so I'd have to try something else. Before I could say anything, Libby spoke again, and she was still fixated on Carolyn.

"They say it's bad luck to speak ill of the dead. Well, she spoke ill of me first."

"What do you mean?"

"I heard you," Libby cried. "I heard you and Lenore and Carolyn talking about me last week at the potluck. You didn't know it, but I heard everything. She was going to ruin it." Libby's normally soft voice was harsh. Her hand fumbled in the bag, and I withdrew further, raising my hands as if they could protect me if she drew out a knife.

Or another letter opener.

"Ruin what?" Even as I spoke, I knew the answer.

"What the colonel was about to ruin. My life. My precious, simple, uncomplicated life." Libby pulled something out of the bag and turned on me. In her hand was an ice pick. A wooden-handled, somewhat rusty ice pick. As dull as the rest of it was, the sharp tip seemed to gleam.

"You know, Reggie. You know, and don't lie. I can tell by the way you're handling me. What do you want? Do you want money to keep my secret? If I pay you off with some of Daddy's money, will you stay quiet?" Libby's face was marked with desperation, her breath coming rapidly, her words spit at me like bullets, her cheeks hot and red.

"I don't know what you mean. I just want you to talk to me." I put my hand out to comfort her. She feinted toward me, but without conviction, so I was able to back off and listen.

"The colonel knew me, Reggie. He knew who I was because he had seen me up close. His friend died in that explosion."

"What explosion?" I asked. I hoped Mac and Shrimp appreciated my efforts to get the whole story while Libby tried to stab me with an ice pick.

Libby's laugh was almost a bark. "You know what explosion. That terrible lab where they were torturing animals! They had to be stopped."

"The animals had been removed from the lab."

"There were always more animals. We had to destroy the lab so they couldn't start their dirty work again." Libby slumped against the lip of the stage. I kept my distance and listened. She wasn't a threat for the moment. "And that poor boy was in the way when our device went off."

"You mean the bomb killed him," I said, correcting the bland way she'd tried to describe the tragedy.

"We risked our own lives to save animals from experimentation over and over," Libby snarled.

"But you're still here."

"Because I found a place where no one knew Elinor Huntington." Libby stood straighter and brought her hand up to point the ice pick at me again. "Until the colonel arrived. He wanted justice. I knew if he turned me in, I'd be spending the rest of my life in prison."

"How do you know he knew who you were?"

"He recognized me. I'd seen him squinting at me in the hall, turning his head from side to side. He'd already made some comments about how I dressed, implying that I should look more professional, and so I thought he was trying to intimidate me about my clothes."

I nodded.

"Then one day I found a photo on my desk."

"The picture that fell out of the book you loaned me," I said.

"He slipped into my room between classes and left it with a note he scribbled: 'Long time, no see.'" Libby sniffed and shook her head to clear the tears gathering in her eyes. "He'd stand beside me in the hall during passing period and whisper stuff to me every day. I heard him say how the animals were safe and sound and I'd helped kill a human being. He told me he knew I wasn't a threat anymore without the gang of hippies I used to hang out with. He said I should be ready for the Feds to show up on my doorstep one day because he was going to take me down."

"But they didn't show up. He was all talk."

"I knew I had to stop him before he could tell." Libby had stopped listening to me, even though she still held the ice pick between us. "I found him backstage that day and I stabbed him. It was that simple. I stabbed him, and I slipped out. It was easy to go unnoticed. Easier, today. There's no one in here but you, and that day the whole cast and crew was here."

I backed up again, and she followed. How much did Mac have to hear?

"What about Carolyn?" I asked to distract her from the weapon.

"Carolyn could have told my secret too, Reggie. A secret isn't a secret once you share it. And mine's been shared out without my permission!" Her voice rose to a scream, and she drew back, aiming at me with the sharp object in her hand. I watched the metallic arc of it headed toward me, and then a flying bundle of flannel and denim landed on top of Libby, taking her to the floor. She struggled, but the sheriff, a former high school tackle, kept her pinned until Shrimp could apply the handcuffs. As Mac stood up, Libby twisted and keened, finally going limp and soundless.

"Are you okay, Reggie?" Mac turned me to him with a hand on each of my shoulders, but kept me at arm's length.

"Yes."

"Is that all? 'Yes'?" Shrimp asked. He looked concerned, an expression I never thought he'd direct at me.

I just nodded.

"Deputy, get her out of here. You've got the car out front. I'll be behind you." Mac sent Shrimp off on the vital errand of putting Libby behind bars. "We'll be calling the *Federales* for this one. I guess they'll be able to take everything off my hands, the colonel and Carolyn both."

I looked into Mac's eyes, and almost didn't register the fact that they were growing closer as Shrimp half-dragged and half-carried Libby out of the auditorium.

"Reggie," Mac whispered, "you did good."

"But I'm still an amateur?"

"Yep. You've got talent, I won't deny it. But you

leave the professional stuff to me. I don't want anything happening to my girl." With that he turned and followed Shrimp out the doors.

I did the same.

CHAPTER TWENTY

I flinched from the feedback on the headset and then heard Rick.

"That's it, folks! Music up. Curtain closed. Prepare for the curtain call."

The stage manager had everything under control, and I sat at the back of the auditorium below the tech booth watching the Italian tomb disappear as the blue velour curtains closed. A lugubrious instrumental came over the speakers, and the curtain opened again. Three weeks after two real-life murders had upset Quanah High School, our students presented a Shakespearean tragedy full of fictional deaths.

The cast came out half a dozen at a time to take their bows on the edge of the stage until the tragic lovers themselves joined hands down center. Chris and Nicole looked at each other and then gestured to the rest of the cast as the applause swelled. Everyone on stage saluted the lighting booth at the back of the auditorium as parents and friends kept clapping. Finally, Chris stepped forward and gestured for quiet.

"We want to take a minute to thank some people," he started. "Shout out to Adam King for letting me take the part of Romeo back. Thanks for letting me rejoin the cast, man!"

Adam, in his tech-crew blacks, had joined everyone else on stage and ducked his head when Chris mentioned him. He tried to take a step back out of the light, but tripped over the bier, where Juliet had spent the last act, and fell prone. He froze, as if no one would notice him if he stayed still.

Chris ignored him. "All of us want to thank Miss Murphy for being the best director ever. Come on down, Murph!"

I shook my head, but he hailed me with a wide gesture and a big grin, so I left my seat and walked down to the front of the stage. As I did, I saw our superintendent, Walter Johnson, slip out the back doors of the auditorium along with the principal. I was happy they'd been at the show, but I also felt like I deserved some support given that our show had been at the center of the two murders.

"I don't know if any director had to play as many roles as ours did putting on this show. I'm no Shakespeare, so I don't think I can really explain how much we appreciate her."

As Chris spoke, the other members of the cast nodded and applauded along with the audience. I saw Nicole, flushed from her turn under the hot lights, her hair slightly askew after dying artfully.

Abby's wimple was gone, and she waved it like a flag, giving me a thumbs up and cocking her head to confirm we were good.

We were.

Lab made a spectacle of himself, jumping up periodically and windmilling an air guitar. He had a solid bunch of fans, mostly freshman girls, gathered at the foot of the stage gazing at him adoringly.

The whole audience had started moving, friends and families toward the stage to greet the actors, others out the back. I nodded at Chris and called out, "Thanks so much for your support, everyone! Come down and say hello to our wonderful thespians!"

And they did.

Abby's parents handed her a bouquet of pink carnations and waved me over for a picture.

"You peaked at the right time, girl," I said, moving close to Abby for the shot.

"Thanks for everything," she replied. "For everything."

"I'm glad we worked through our little disagreement," Jessica Beamer commented. She scrolled through the pictures and nodded in satisfaction when she saw one she liked. "She thinks the world of you."

Abby rolled her eyes and mouthed, "I mean it, but my mom's kind of extra."

I nodded and waved them off.

Chris's mom, Ginny, came to me while Chris was busy signing programs for the crush of people who stood around him when he sat on the edge of the stage.

"Your boy did a great job!" I said, reaching out to shake her hand.

She pulled me in for a hug instead. "Thank you, Miss Murphy. Thank you for giving him a chance. I didn't know he would be so good, and he's so happy to be up there."

"How are you doing?" I asked when we'd pulled back. Looking at her, I saw a sadness that I thought had always been there.

"We're hanging in." She looked over at her son. "I thought we'd move back East where my family is, but now I'm torn. He seems to have found a new family here."

"I'd hate to lose him."

"Maybe I can hang on for another year so he can graduate from Quanah. He deserves that much, after all he went through with his father. I could never talk about it, and Chris wouldn't, but life at home with the colonel wasn't easy."

I just nodded.

"He never laid a finger on either of us, but he was very demanding," she said, leaning in close and keeping her voice low. "He didn't understand what Chris got from your drama class, but I can see what it's done for him. God rest his soul, but now that he's gone, I think Chris can finally be who he was meant to be."

"I'm happy he found that here."

Ginny slipped away, and I heard her tell Chris, "Don't be late."

And then she was gone.

"Wonderful show!" Lenore stepped up. Will had come with her, but he hung back even as he held her hand. She patted my shoulder and said, "I still don't believe reading Romeo and Juliet is the best way to introduce these freshmen to the Bard, but seeing it live, well, maybe that will show them what all the fuss is about. Do you have to stay around for a cast party or can you stop by for a nightcap?"

"The kids are all going to IHOP in Owasso, I think. I need to clear the theater and shut down all the lights." Lenore's offer was tempting, but the only company I wanted after I shooed everyone out of the auditorium was Gus. I couldn't tell Lenore I preferred my cat's company to hers, though, so I just said, "I'll pass on the nightcap this time."

"See you Monday morning then."

"No, you won't! Spring break, remember?" I said.

"You're right. I'm such a creature of habit I'd forgotten we get a whole week to ourselves. Well, let me know if you feel at loose ends, and we can get up to some trouble together." Lenore waved as Will pulled her away.

"What kind of trouble?" a voice in my ear said. A deep baritone voice.

I twirled around and came face to face with Mac. "Like I'm going to tell anyone, Sheriff!"

"Want me to hang around while you close up?"

"No, I'm fine."

The crowd had thinned out until only a couple of parents waited for their kids. Most of the cast had gone backstage to get rid of their costumes before returning to the house to meet up with others and leave. I felt the adrenaline of the show ebbing.

"Part of me is sad Libby isn't here. Is that weird?"

"No, I don't think so. The Libby you knew was excited to be a part of this. She loved these kids just like you do. Too bad Elinor Huntington had made some bad choices."

"I have to think about it that way. Libby was sweet, and tough on the inside, but there was nothing sweet about the woman who killed Colonel Slayton. What a waste."

"She'll be gone a long time. Maybe she'll find a way to be useful inside."

I nodded. My throat had tightened up thinking about how the tranquil history teacher I'd known for so long had turned out to be someone completely different. She'd taught kids how non-violence had changed the world year after year, but when her world was threatened, she'd resorted to murder. It wasn't enough she'd killed the colonel, a retired soldier who knew something about violence, but she'd killed Carolyn, the sweet, simple woman who'd never threatened anyone. I shook a little, and my eyes filled with tears.

Mac reached out for my hands. I looked around, making sure everyone had left before I let him take them and pull me close. He brushed the tears away from my eyes. "Remember she's the exception, not the rule. Not everyone you like is faking who they are."

"I'm happy to hear you say that."

He grinned. "Now, I don't think I want you telling tales to anyone about what we've got planned for this week. Even to Lenore."

"I don't kiss and tell."

"There's going to be kissing? Don't want you to scare the fish."

"I'll stay out of your way while you're fishing. They'll never know I'm there. I'll just put my sun hat on and pull out my book while you pull 'em in."

"Hauling my old boat out on the lake every day will give us plenty of time to get to know one another, won't it?"

I nodded, and the vision of the sunny lake dried up the tears that hadn't had a chance to fall.

Deviled Eggs

Reg usually takes these deviled eggs to school potlucks because they're the simplest thing to make. Well, that's not exactly true. It's simpler to unwrap a block of cream cheese, place it on a pretty serving plate, pour a half a jar of pepper jelly over it, and set out an opened box of snack crackers to accompany it. However, everyone seems to love her deviled eggs, so there you are.

I started the list of ingredients with the eggs already boiled and peeled. Opinions differ about how to best boil an egg. Of late, I have come to depend on my Instant Pot, but Reg does it the old-fashioned way, on the stove. She finds starting the eggs in cold water, bringing it to a boil, and then slapping a lid on the pan and removing it from the heat is effective, but you do you.

Pro-tip: a deviled egg plate is a delightful shower gift, and Reg has found they make a nice collectible as well—so that you're not wondering what exactly you're looking for if you find yourself in an antique store or flea market.

Ingredients:
12 eggs, hardboiled and peeled
1/2 cup mayonnaise
2 teaspoons yellow mustard
Salt and Pepper to taste
Paprika, for sprinkling

Method 1:
1. Cut each egg in half. Place the yolks in a medium-sized bowl and the intact white halves on a serving plate.
2. Mash the yolks with a fork and then add the mayonnaise, mustard, salt, and pepper. Blend thoroughly.
3. Fill the cavity of each egg white with heaping teaspoons of the yolk mixture.
4. Sprinkle paprika artistically over the completed eggs.

Method 2:
1. Cut each egg in half. Place the yolks in a gallon-sized plastic storage bag and the intact white halves on a serving plate.
2. Add the mayonnaise, mustard, salt and pepper to the yolks in the bag. Squeeze the bag to thoroughly blend the ingredients.
3. Snip off a corner of the bag, and deploy the yolk mixture like frosting to fill the whites.
4. Sprinkle paprika artistically over the completed eggs.

Acknowledgements

While no one but the author can pound the keyboard, the many people who inspired, guided, and responded to multiple drafts were always there in my head and I appreciate their role in making Reg's world what it is.

The author Richard Brautigan once said, "My teachers could have been Jesse James for all the time they stole from me." I approach every day in the classroom and in rehearsal with that in mind, and try not to waste the precious time my students and I have together. I hope the students who chose to spend their time working with me over the years know how much I appreciate them. I have learned from them and hope my affection for them is clear in this work.

Terri Kruse, my stalwart Beta reader, deserves thanks for taking up another manuscript and giving me such valuable feedback! You made me feel like a rock star while ruthlessly pointing out all the problems that needed attention. Jeri Westmoreland, a known fan of the cozy genre, was also a valuable resource, as was fellow cozy author Faith Wylie. I appreciate you both taking the time to read Reg's story. In addition, my sister, who is several sorts of an artist herself, was a wonderful first reader and I always welcome her support and her advice.

Finally, thank you to my husband, Keith. His belief in me as a writer has been instrumental in moving me forward on so many projects. He tells a good story and pushes me to write all of mine down.

About the Author

Jennifer Oakley Denslow is a career speech and theater educator with a passion for stories. When she isn't using every spare second to pen her latest novel, she can be found coaching her debate team and working with young actors to create the emotional experiences for which theater was meant.

Jennifer's first book, the historical novel *An Ignorance of Means*, is available on Amazon. You can find more about Jennifer's work on her website by scanning the QR code below. or visiting www.jenniferoakleydenslow.com .

Made in the USA
Columbia, SC
02 April 2021